I0623983

Releasing the Beast

The Imperfect Shifter Series – Book 1

by

Amelia Hopegood
Published by Amelia Hopegood

Chapter 1

Ben

I wonder if I'll ever stop longing to feel like I belong? To find that person who understands and needs you as much as you need them – my fated mate. I would probably only mess it up anyway; it's not as if I had a good example to follow. It's safer to remain alone.

I suppose.

*

The snow felt crisp and cool under my heavily padded paws. My animal might not be a native of snow-capped mountains, but over the years, like me, it had come to associate the snow with freedom and escape. It embraced this as I ran across the white snow, flurries still falling as we surged deeper into the whiteout – it was liberating.

Running without fear or restraint is one of the few joys in life that I'd never thought I'd be able to experience after I first left home. Feeling safe should never be underestimated, for it was a pleasure I'd come to realise wasn't a guarantee in this world.

We ran as one, man and beast linked, wishing for the same – liberty – and almost taking flight across wide open spaces as we enjoyed our freedom. Hot breath billowed out of my mouth as I covered as much distance as possible. There were only certain times I could risk such an outpouring of energy; the highlands of Scotland were wonderfully remote. Walkers and skiers sometimes had a bad habit of exploring the more remote peaks, but I had learned over the years that certain times of day and poorer weather conditions were better, as there was less risk of discovery.

My stripes would stand out against the brilliant white of the snow, but my speed and heightened senses meant that usually I noticed people far earlier than they would spot me. Then I would veer off, and the extra adrenaline would carry me even faster away from discovery. It was an exhilarating experience.

Pausing at the summit of a peak, I let out a roar that echoed off the surrounding mountainsides. I was unconstrained from everyday life and it felt wonderful.

An hour later, I'd returned to my log cabin by the sides of Loch Einich. There were only six other cabins, positioned far enough apart to be private. Don't get me wrong – I like people, but I also want my space, and in the five years I've owned this cabin, I've gained some much-needed inner peace.

Noticing a vehicle I didn't recognise, it was clear that the number four cabin was let out. It was the only cabin which was a holiday let, and there was a steady stream of people throughout the year who came to enjoy the peace and tranquillity of the area. There wasn't enough to do to tempt the hen and stag parties that might cause problems in the area or get too rowdy; instead, it attracted nature lovers and walkers.

I was about to walk into my own accommodation when I heard a sound which stopped my progress. My tiger was on full alert, bristling to shift as it sensed danger. The sound I'd heard was a growl, I was sure of it, and it was coming from the newly let lodge.

Damping down the urge to shift, I crept towards the other lodge. I could be almost as silent in human form as I was as a tiger. My senses were working, and I soon picked up the scent of an animal. Bear. But there was something else, or someone else, and that person was afraid and begging whoever had shifted into a dangerous animal to change back. From the sounds of it, the bear wasn't co-operating.

Reaching the outside of the cabin, I moved to the door and listened. It sounded as if the animal was lurching around the space inside, knocking things over and growling the whole time. The sounds were more of distress than anger, but there was something else which made me pause: the most attractive scent which had ever made my nose twitch. It was a mixture of vanilla and jasmine, and it stirred something deep and hidden inside me.

I tried to concentrate on what was going on rather than enjoying the scent I could smell, as a woman's voice was pleading with the animal, and she sounded distressed.

"Please, Nathan, change back. You can't be seen here. We're in no danger now, honestly – please change," she repeated over and over again.

I waited, unmoving. I could leave them to it, but I didn't want the bear to turn on whoever was inside with him, which, from the sounds of it, he could do at any time. She sounded like a young woman, so I presumed the bear was her husband. As much as I didn't want to antagonise a full-grown bear, I couldn't leave someone at risk either, even if they didn't smell as delicious as this person did.

Without warning, the door of the lodge burst open and a medium-sized brown bear lurched out of the open doorway. Immediately sensing me, he turned and, with a snarl, launched himself in my direction.

My tiger was roaring inside, but I managed to jump out of danger while maintaining my human form. I'd realised in time that this was a young bear, and if I shifted, my tiger would rip him apart with ease. No. I couldn't change at this point for his sake. I was in no real danger, not enough to reveal myself in tiger form anyway, no matter that my beast disagreed with me completely.

"Whoa, there!" I said quietly, hands up in an act of surrender. "Shh, there's no need to be angry. No one's going to hurt you."

A woman followed the bear out and put her face in her hands at the sight of me. Now, call me vain if you like, but hiding faces wasn't the usual reaction I received when first meeting an attractive woman. I hoped for my ego that it was the situation causing her distress.

"It's Nathan, isn't it? Easy boy, there's nothing to get yourself upset about here," I continued to soothe, while the bear stood on his hind legs, seeming to weigh me up. He was as tall as me, over six feet in height, but I could see by his build that he was still a young cub. Probably a boy reaching puberty, which was always a difficult time for a shifter. "Why don't you relax and shift into human form, and we can talk about what upset you to cause your change? I'm not going to hurt you, but I am freezing to death out here and would appreciate going somewhere warm."

The bear tilted his head, seeming to consider my words. It was good that he could obviously understand me. When some first started to change, it was as if they were completely separate from their human side. It made training and becoming attuned to the two beings living within a person more difficult. I was grateful that this one appeared more in sync with his animal.

After a pause, the bear got down onto all fours and the change from beast to human took place. He crumpled onto the snowy ground when he'd fully reverted, the motion of shifting exhausting him.

The young woman and I reached his naked form at the same time. She fell to the ground, her concern overwhelming her, her jeans getting wet in the snow.

"Nathan! Nathan! Wake up!" she urged. As I placed my hand on her shoulder, she looked up in alarm. Frightened hazel eyes stared back at me. "Thank you for your help. I can take it from here," she said.

"Don't wake him; let him recover his strength. I guess his shifting is all new, so let him be. Let me carry him inside for you. It's too cold out here for him to spend any time in his current state."

"I can manage —"

"Yes, you probably can, but I can help," I said, no longer waiting for her permission, but bending down and scooping the boy into my arms. He couldn't be any older than twelve or thirteen. Poor lad, it seemed he was only at the very beginning of his journey.

Walking into the cabin, I paused for a second. Nathan had trashed it, but it was also filled with the almost overwhelming scent of the woman. My tiger was preening himself, ready to claim a mate, even though we'd been in her company for mere minutes. Getting myself and my tiger under control, I continued over to a sofa, laid the still-sleeping boy down, and grabbed the throw that was over the back of the piece of furniture. Covering him up, I turned to the woman, who was still watching me with suspicion.

"I'm Ben," I said, holding out my hand. "I own number six across the way."

"Thank you for your help. Please leave."

I'm not one unable to take a hint, but there was obviously a problem here. A shifter like Nathan could hurt a human unintentionally, and that would cause a problem for the whole shifting community. Also, I could detect fear and uncertainty in this woman. While normally I would guard my privacy and hers, I couldn't leave her to deal with an unpredictable shifter, however young he was, no matter that my tiger was constantly whispering *mate*.

"I'd like to stay and give you a hand to clear up."

"There's no need."

"I know there isn't, but I'd like to anyway."

"Do you never take no for an answer?" she snapped, running her hand through her hair. It was a rich dark brown with a natural sheen, falling back into place when her fingers had released it, which did nothing to subdue the feelings swirling inside both me and my tiger.

"Regularly, but in this case, I think I can offer practical help, and you look like you need it. Why be stubborn about it?"

"I'm not being. I wanted to be private."

"That makes two of us, but there are times when we all need a hand. I think this is one of those moments. Why don't we start again? I'm Ben. I only want to help; I promise I am no threat to either of you. Hello." I wasn't usually so alpha male, but the boy was obviously out of his depth and however much she didn't like to admit it, so was she. Ok, that statement was a bit alpha male, but it wasn't intended to be – I just knew people. Shifters usually could read a non-shifter as easily as picking a magazine up and flicking through its pages, the non-verbal body movements being clear to any beast needing to stay alive in a harsh world.

I could see the internal struggle she was having with herself. She probably didn't realise what she was revealing, but I could see the moment she decided to let me stay, and had to suppress a smile when she sighed. "Hello, I'm Kerry," she answered and, albeit reluctantly, shook my hand.

"Looks like you had fun before Nathan went outside. Shall we get started?"

"There really is no need. Thank you for bringing Nathan in, but you really don't need to help."

I wasn't surprised at her response. It was clear she didn't want me anywhere near her or her relation, which would usually suit me, but there was something about them which tugged at my usual instinct to walk away and made me stay. I started to pick up some of the cushions which had landed on the floor.

She was acting like a frightened animal, but was human, I was sure of it. I shouldn't be curious about her story – I was here for solitude and freedom – but the police officer in me was hard to shake off. No, that was unfair; it wasn't just my training that was stirring my interest, it was her large hazel eyes in a pretty face and her overwhelming emotion of fear, which stirred my compassion, that, and the fact that her scent was screaming 'mate' at me in addition to my tiger.

Sighing, she pushed her glasses up her nose. "I should be gracious and just say thank you, shouldn't I? We've had a long journey and I'm tired. Your help would be appreciated."

"Good. Let's get this place back to how it was and then we can be calm when Nathan wakes up."

"No! I mean, it would be best if you weren't here when he wakes."

I'd thought a little of the worry had gone from her expression when she accepted my help, but it was now fully back in place. Smiling, I began to plump up the cushions and move some books that had been scattered across the room. At least it didn't look like there had been much damage, just disruption. "He's going through a difficult time; he might have questions, and I can probably give him some answers and tips which will help him in future." I was betraying too much, but she seemed completely out of her depth and I couldn't remain quiet.

"You're a shifter," she said and sank into a chair in defeat, taking her glasses off and rubbing her hand over her face.

"I am. Is that a problem?" I didn't know whether to laugh or be offended. She was with a shifter and yet prejudiced against my kind? That didn't make sense at all.

"Yes. No. I don't know."

Leaving the tidying, I sat down, but kept some distance between us. "I don't belong to a pack – I'm a lone animal. I know I'm being a bit bull-headed about hanging around, but I'm no threat to you." In fact, the way my tiger and I were both responding to this woman meant that the only urge she was stirring in me was to protect her. Not unsurprising when looking at the career I'd chosen. I upheld the law of the land and protected people. The savage instincts of my tiger were sometimes in conflict with my profession, but the human side of me was always in control at those times.

My words had caused a slight smile, but it soon disappeared. A shame, for in that couple of seconds, she looked younger than she appeared when frowning, her face pinched with worry. "It would be best for us all if you left and forgot you'd ever seen us. We'll be gone in a day or two," Kerry said, putting her glasses back on and setting her shoulders.

And that was the best piece of advice I would probably ever be given. Needless to say, I ignored it.

Chapter 2

Kerry

Only I could be trying to escape and run into another shifter, I cursed inwardly as his amber eyes watched me intently. Add the fact that he was absolutely stunning to look at – over six feet tall, broad athletic shoulders and a face which would be quite at home on some renaissance masterpiece – and it seemed the gods were laughing at me. Especially because he seemed nice, but then again, many people did on first meeting, and only when it was too late did they reveal their true selves.

Nathan had been agitated all the way up; it was a miracle his transformation hadn't occurred in one of the service stations we'd stopped at on the way to the Cairngorms. My bladder would probably never recover from being forced to wait to the last possible moment before we stopped. I'd wanted to leave the least trail we could in these days of being constantly picked up by the technology around us. We were probably already on too many CCTV images.

New phone, new car, and accommodation booked on a new laptop in an internet café – that was all I could do to try and delay being found. I wasn't sure if any of it would work, but I was determined that Nathan wouldn't be harmed because of what he was. I'd made a promise and I was going to keep it.

Ben just looked at me when I'd finished my speech, those large amber eyes seeming to take in my every movement. There wasn't suspicion in his expression; it seemed to be genuine concern. For some strange reason, I longed to lean into him and let him take control and ease my fears, which I felt like I'd been living with for so long that I wasn't convinced I'd ever be able to relax again. Ignoring my foolishness, I responded to him far more coolly than the old me would have done.

Instead of taking offence at my snappishness, he just looked at me with sympathy. "I can offer Nathan some advice which will help him. If there's only the two of you and you are not a shifter, you can't imagine how confusing it is when the changes start."

It was a kind gesture he was offering, and I did appreciate it, because I certainly didn't know how best to help the boy who now relied on me for everything. "He's a little different from normal shifters," I said. I don't know what I expected from my words, but unfortunately for me, the shifter who was sitting opposite me was no fool, nor was he easily persuaded to leave well alone.

"Then he probably needs my help even more. Come on, let's get this place straightened and you can put the kettle on," Ben said, standing and starting to pick things up off the floor once more.

"Why are you being so nice? You don't know us and you'll never see us after tomorrow." I was actually booked in the lodge for two nights, but I decided we couldn't remain in this area for that long, not with a helpful neighbour around. It was too risky. The more people who saw us, the more we risked discovery – a pity then that in other circumstances I would have liked very much to spend more time with this man. Trying to stop the sigh from escaping, I realised that the whole situation was far too complicated for someone who had, until recently, enjoyed your average, mundane life.

Ben seemed to weigh up what he was going to say next, and even though I cursed my weakness in still wanting to trust someone, I longed to hear something reassuring from him. Blasted pathetic specimen that I was.

"I'm trying to help because we all feel out of our depth at some point, and it's a bit easier when you can curse at someone else who has already been there and done it."

"I've done a lot of cursing lately."

"Trust me, it feels better when you are cursing along with someone else. Now come on, I'm not doing all the work." He threw a cushion at me and I caught it with a reluctant laugh. The sound sounded strange to me – I couldn't remember the last time I'd laughed.

I stood, throwing caution to the wind in letting him stay, and followed his lead, trying to right the destruction Nathan had caused.

After the lodge was back to its pristine self, I put the coffee machine on and inserted a pod. Handing a steaming cup to Ben, I added another pod to the machine for myself. I doubted I needed any caffeine to add to my frayed nerves and alert status, but I needed something to keep my hands occupied, or they would betray my inner anxiety.

"How long does he normally sleep after a change?" Ben asked.

"It varies depending on where we are, but it can be a couple of hours," I admitted.

"Would you like me to come back when he's awake? I don't want to crowd you now that things are back in order. People who come to these lodges usually do so to escape and enjoy the peace and tranquillity, not to be bombarded by nosey neighbours," he said with a smile. "I know I was a little full on at the start, but it was just to assist with the mess, honestly."

"Is that why you've bought one of the lodges? For an escape?" It was a strange thing for him to say. I would have thought he would be welcomed wherever he went.

"Oh yes. I like to be in wide-open spaces as much as possible. It's a pity I can't afford to give up work, or I'd live up here, or somewhere like it."

His words struck me as strange. He had so far seemed very sociable, which went against the longing in his voice. "Would you not be lonely?" I couldn't help asking. I knew for a fact that Nathan and I would probably be lonely in our future, but if that was the only way to ensure Nathan's safety and have some semblance of a life, then it was worth it.

"Perhaps, but I can always seek out company when I need to."

Why did his words make me bristle? I immediately thought he was referring to women by the tone of his voice. Jealous of a man I didn't know? Things were getting desperate if that was the case. I'd best put all those kinds of feelings firmly to one side, I cursed inwardly. It was going to be a nun's life for me from now on. I had to focus on Nathan; nothing else mattered. For the first time since accepting it, I felt sadness about my decision, and the change in sentiment was due to the man I'd just met.

"Surely you have to be sociable for work? What is it you do?"

"I'm taking a career break from my day job and trying to set up a business with a couple of like-minded friends. If it works out, I might not go back to the daily commute."

Nathan stirred and we both looked across at him. His big brown eyes opened slowly, focusing on the room and then seeking me out. "Kerry?" he asked in confusion as he saw Ben. Trying to sit up, he rubbed his head.

"Headache, Nathan?" Ben asked, crossing to where Nathan lay and sitting down on the chair opposite him. He was close, but not close enough to intimidate him. "I always got a headache after a change when they first began."

Nathan scrambled to the rear of the sofa he'd been lying on. I could tell he was afraid of Ben and crossed the room towards him. "Try and keep calm, Nathan," I soothed. I cursed my inability to insist that this stranger leave us. Now, Nathan was in danger of changing again while he was still recovering from the last time. It was unfair that he be punished for my patheticness in being unable to rebuff an attractive man. Some protector I was.

"Who are you?" Nathan asked, watching Ben closely.

"I'm just like you," Ben answered quietly. He was very still and his body language was relaxed.

"There's hardly anyone like me," Nathan answered, and I closed my eyes. He couldn't reveal his true self, or we would need to get away quickly, which I really didn't want to do, and I also did not wish to examine the reasons why at this point.

"I'm not a bear, that's true," Ben said. "How long have you been shifting?"

"Nearly two years, but there wasn't much shifting for the first few months."

"You'll definitely still get the headaches and fuzzy head then, won't you?"

Nathan nodded, but he'd glanced at me and I could tell by his expression that he understood I didn't want him revealing more.

"Nathan could do with a couple of painkillers and a warm drink. Do you have anything like hot chocolate? It's more soothing and helps ease the feelings of sickness," Ben asked me.

"Yes, I have." I'd bought most of the groceries at the supermarket when I made my final shop before we left, trying to prevent the need for us to shop anywhere else, again trying to reduce our chances of being seen. I busied myself with making the drink and then walked across to give it to Nathan, also giving him the painkillers Ben had suggested. "Take these," I said gently.

"It will get easier, but you need rest after every change in these early days," Ben said to Nathan. "Have you got a mentor?"

Nathan shook his head in the negative and Ben looked at me, a question in his amber eyes.

"He's the first shifter in the family." That wasn't quite true and Ben would know it wasn't, but I refused to start trying to explain our background. We'd revealed too much already.

Ben seemed to assess me, and I grew uncomfortable under his scrutiny. I tried to keep my expression bland, but I could feel my eyes giving myself away and I closed them in frustration.

"Every shifter needs a mentor when the changes start. It can be a frightening time, and lessons need to be taught about how to control the shifts. Do they come on when you're upset, or out of sorts?" he asked Nathan.

Bless him, Nathan shrugged, trying not to give anything away. It shouldn't have been like this – Nathan should have had everything he needed to make the transition from boy to shifter, and would have had if life had been normal, but it wasn't. I felt so sorry for him that I couldn't offer him anything useful at this time. He'd suffered so much already. At least now I knew he needed to rest and that shifting would get easier for him.

Watching the uncertainty on Nathan's face, I took a breath. What I was about to do was a risk, but I was prepared to do it for his sake. We needed some help, and meeting Ben might just have been providence.

"Could you give us some tips as to what would be useful to Nathan?" I asked. I smiled at the surprised but hopeful look in Nathan's expression and knew I'd done the right thing. He was struggling with everything, but he wasn't asking for help because he understood the predicament we were in. It was unfair that he was feeling so lost.

"I could. How long are you around for?" Ben asked.

"We leave tomorrow," I said firmly, shooting a glance at Nathan. We had planned to stay two nights, but I couldn't risk any other information we were trying to keep hidden being discovered by Ben.

"Let me join you this evening and we can go through a few practicalities," Ben said. "I can give you some basic tricks which might help." He stood and looked at me. "Wherever you are going, if you're staying there for a while, I'd look for someone to mentor him. It's crucial at the stage he's at."

"I have got something arranged already," I answered honestly. I did have, he didn't need to know precisely what.

"That's good. I'll leave you be and let Nathan rest further, but I'll see you about seven if that's ok?"

"Yes, that's good for us. Thank you," I responded.

"You're very welcome. I'll see you later."

I followed Ben to the door and waited until he'd crossed back to his own lodge before I closed the door and leaned against it for support. Closing my eyes for a second, I cursed my choice of stopping place. It had seemed remote enough, but only my poor luck could land us with another shifter.

"Aunty Kerry?" Nathan asked as I remained prone, leaning against the door. "I'm sorry I couldn't stop the change."

Immediately reacting to the sadness and uncertainty in his voice, I crossed to my nephew. "I know you couldn't. From what Ben has said, it seems what's happening to you is a perfectly normal part of becoming a full shifter."

"But I'm not normal, am I?" he asked, uncertainty being replaced with fear.

Taking hold of his hands, I sat down next to him. "I've told you that there are others like you. They're the ones we're going to find. They've promised to protect you and offer you a good life. I'm going to do my best to get you there safely." If it was the last thing I did, I had to reach those who were like Nathan; it was his only chance at a normal life.

"Will you stay with me when we reach them?" he asked. He looked so young sometimes, even younger than his thirteen years, and my heart broke for him.

"I will stay for as long as you need me," I promised. The conversations I'd had with those who were prepared to offer him sanctuary had warned me that there might come a point when I'd lose him completely. I had cried for a full eight hours when I'd been told that. It wasn't bad enough to lose my baby sister, but I now had to face the prospect of losing the only person who linked me directly to her. Every time I looked at Nathan, I was reminded of Viv – he had the same deep brown eyes and wide smile she'd had. I now knew that one day I might lose that connection, and it meant that as often as I could, I would sit and look at Nathan, trying to imprint his features more deeply onto my memory. I needed it for his memory and hers.

"Thanks, Aunty Kerry. Can I go to sleep now? I'm still tired."

"Of course you can, sweetheart. I'll make us something to eat for when you wake up. Sleep well, little wolf."

Nathan smiled at my pet name for him before closing his eyes and falling into a deep sleep. Walking over to the kitchen area of the lodge, I started to pull food out of the fridge quietly. For a couple of hours, we could try to pretend life was normal and safe.

I knew it wouldn't last, but I had to try and relax whilst it did.

Chapter 3

Ben

Walking over to the lodge at seven, my tiger was almost pacing around my insides. "Yes, I know you think it's a bad idea, but he needs help and she's out of her depth."

He was slightly consoled that we would be spending the evening in the company of an attractive woman, which was the only reason he wasn't making life extremely uncomfortable for me. He was frustrated with my lack of attempts to find a mate; I was now thirty-five and long overdue for setting my sights on continuing my lineage. He failed to understand how much the thought of bringing a child into this world terrified me. Why would I want to inflict such pain and rejection as I had faced onto someone I cared about deeply? It was a parent's role to protect, and I wouldn't be able to take away every bad experience. A tiger was not an easy animal to live with, even less so with the wrong community around it.

I was able to reassure myself that I would be able to help a young boy at the start of his journey and spend an evening in the company of a pretty woman, which would hopefully keep my tiger quiet. I had to push aside the feeling that she was the only woman who had produced in either of us the feeling of meeting our true mate; now was not the time.

Kerry smiled as she opened the door, which was something of an advance from the afternoon. There was still a wariness about her and I didn't blame her for it – I was very much a stranger in their midst.

Nathan was sitting at the breakfast bar, eating a large piece of cake. He looked at me, openly wary of my presence. He wasn't changing, which was a good thing; it seemed he had a little control over his beast.

"I always get the urge to eat a ton of sweet stuff after I've shifted," I said, smiling. Handing over a large bar of chocolate, I laughed at the expression on Nathan's face. "Don't eat it now. It looks like you've plenty to go at already. Use this when you run out of cake."

"Coffee?" Kerry asked, moving to the coffee machine.

"Please. Are you able to constantly communicate with your bear?" I asked Nathan. There was no point in not getting straight to business when they'd be leaving tomorrow, a thought that for some reason I didn't relish. Usually, I loved it when the lodges were empty.

"Sometimes," Nathan said, but he looked down, hiding something.

I continued without questioning him. "That will increase. At the moment, your animal is able to force its will on you. It's perfectly normal – it's only just woken up and wants to assert its authority, but you need to be the one in control. You were worried when I came in. How did you stop yourself from shifting?"

Nathan looked surprised at my words. "You knew I wanted to change?"

"Yes. I could see your struggle."

"I just kept saying no, no, no, in my head," he admitted.

"It's clear your animal listens to you, which is a good sign," I assured him. "Mine responds to me, although sometimes my hands start turning into claws before I manage to stop it from taking over into a full shift." Kerry handed me a coffee, which I accepted and turned my attention back to Nathan. "Although it can be useful just letting the person who is causing your upset see what you are – it very often makes them listen more carefully."

"Really?" Nathan asked. "That would be so cool. What are you? Where is your pack?"

It had taken so little for his wariness to ease, I wondered if he'd ever been able to speak to anyone about his situation. "I don't have a pack. I'm a lone animal, although I do have friends who are the same as me."

"I thought everyone had to have a pack," Nathan said.

"With an animal like a wolf, it's easy. They're pack animals, but we're not all the same. Some of us would be loners in the wild, so we are as shifters, when we shift, of course. We still belong to our family as humans," I explained. I missed the part that said unless you had a family like mine.

"What are you?" Kerry asked.

Here we go, I groaned silently. The shutters would come down and I would be spending the rest of the evening alone. "A tiger."

"A tiger?" Nathan exclaimed. "No way! I've never seen a tiger shifter before!"

"There aren't many of us around," I said, watching Kerry's face. Her wariness had increased, but to her credit, she hadn't stepped away from me, which was the usual reaction when revealing what my animal was.

"I wish I could pick what animal we were." Nathan brought my attention back to him.

"Every species has its upsides and downsides," I admitted. "Not accepting your animal won't help when you are trying to learn to live with it. You don't want it resenting you for wishing to be something you're not."

"If only it was that simple," Kerry muttered, but she'd turned away from me, so I knew she was talking to herself. A pity for her that my hearing is far better than that of any human.

Nathan had finished eating, and although he looked at the chocolate longingly, he didn't open it.

"Shall we practise some techniques which will help give you some sort of control?" I asked.

"Please," he said, jumping off the stool and moving to the spacious lounge area.

Kerry stayed in the kitchen area, but watched us the whole time. I spent the next two hours instructing

Nathan on how to try to control the urges his animal was sending out to him. He was eager to learn, but by the end of our session, he flopped onto the sofa, clearly exhausted.

"You've had a busy day," I said, ruffling his hair. "That's enough for now. Practise every day what we've gone through and it will get easier. Once you get a full-time mentor, he or she will be able to go through everything else you need to know."

"Thanks," Nathan said.

"There is one other thing." I glanced at Kerry. "If you're moving on tomorrow, it would be of benefit if I called for Nathan early – really early – then he could shift safely with me and we could go for some exercise over the mountains."

"No!" Kerry said immediately.

"His animal is struggling for freedom; if it has some time each day to be released, it will be more stable for the rest of the day. Nathan will be able to sleep while you drive, and you can relax knowing that at the slightest surprise, he won't suddenly shift." I don't know if my explanation was enough to convince her, but I was speaking the truth.

"Aunty Kerry – err Kerry, please," Nathan said, flushing a little at revealing some personal information which he had clearly been told to keep to himself. She was his aunt? That led to a whole set of other questions, many of which didn't reflect too well on Kerry.

Waiting, I watched as a myriad of emotions passed over her face, but she shook her head at Nathan. "I'm sorry, but it has to be a no."

Nathan looked as if he was about to argue, so I thought it prudent to interrupt. There was no point causing angst between the two of them; there was clearly more going on than I knew. My policing background and my need to be cautious around people wanted to demand that I be told what was really going on, but coming across so heavy-handed wasn't going to help either of them. I also had the feeling that Kerry was a decent person, and my gut instinct was rarely wrong.

"Don't worry about it. I just thought it might help. Try to shift for a little while before you start your lessons with your mentor," I said to Nathan. "It will help settle your animal's urges, making it more responsive to you. Eventually, you'll be able to call all the shots." I had to suppress a smile as my tiger almost roared with indignation at my words, but I rubbed my chest, soothing my beast. "I'll be leaving at five in the morning. I like to go out before the early skiers head out. If you change your mind," I said to Kerry, "just let him be at my car by five."

"Thanks for the offer, but it's best if we just set off early on our journey," she said stiffly.

"No problem. I'll say my goodbyes now then. Good luck, Nathan," I said and walked to the door. Kerry had followed me, her arms wrapped around her middle, and I can honestly say it wasn't just my tiger who wanted to wrap his paws around her to comfort her. I stuffed my hands into my jeans pockets to prevent me from acting rashly.

"Thank you for your help today," she said, opening the door.

"You're welcome, and if you need anything before you leave here, please let me know."

"We'll be fine."

"I'm sure you will be, but don't be afraid to ask. I hope you both have a good journey."

"Bye," Kerry said and closed the door.

Smiling slightly, I headed over to my own lodge. There was no nonsense with Kerry, which I liked. She was set on her plan, whatever it was and wherever they were going, and that was it. I liked her independence; she was no shifter, but she would be a perfect tigress.

My own tiger agreed and grumbled for an hour at my lack of action in trying to secure Kerry as a mate. Sometimes it wasn't easy having half of you who was almost caveman-like in his attitudes. It's what caused some of the antagonism with the human population when some shifters gave in to their baser responses. I wasn't going to be one of those men, though – I'd grown up being constantly reminded of how badly someone can behave, and I was determined to be different.

Chapter 4

Kerry

Hitting my alarm, I blinked in the strange room, needing a moment to gather my conscious thoughts and let my brain come out of the fog that threatened to envelop it and send me back to sleep. The comfortable bed, down quilt, and pillows didn't help; they felt like cotton wool was cuddling me and tempting me to succumb to my dreams.

Eventually forcing myself out of bed, I padded over to the ensuite. Glancing in the mirror, I grimaced – the disturbed night of sleep last night showed in my red-rimmed eyes and the dark rings underneath. I could see them plainly, even without my glasses on. I was usually pale-skinned, but I could pass as a ghost this morning. Resting my forehead on the mirror, I let my breath steam the glass.

The argument with Nathan last night had been hard. I had tried to make him understand why I'd refused permission for him to go out with Ben. It was just too risky, but I hated myself for restricting him when I knew the chance for him to be with another shifter who seemed to be a good guy was what he longed to do. I'd watched him with Ben as he'd soaked up all the information Ben had thrown at him; it had been so bittersweet. Viv would have been pleased and proud to see how eager Nathan was and how quick to learn. He was going to be amazing, if only I could get him to safety.

The usual panic and anxiety fluttered in my stomach, but I tried to force it down before it started to affect my breathing. If that happened, I would be of no use to anyone. Once I'd made sure Nathan was well settled, I would be able to relax and these episodes would ease, I hoped.

After taking a long shower, I felt refreshed and ready for breakfast and the day ahead. It would have been nice to spend the day in this area, I thought as I opened the curtains in my bedroom. The view was of the loch, with some bird skimming over the surface, no doubt in search of its own breakfast. It was so peaceful and tranquil; I could see why Ben liked it so much. It was about as far away as you could get, yet in reality, it was only a short drive to amenities, should you need them.

Ben. I felt guilty in admitting it, but my inability to sleep last night had also been due to pondering about him, not just worrying about Nathan. He seemed like a nice person, yet he was effectively doing what we were doing – hiding out in the middle of nowhere. I wondered about him and was curious as to why he seemed so alone. I could see he missed absolutely nothing that went on, those amber eyes taking everything in, but there was also a hint of loneliness about him. Strange if he was actually the friendly, handsome – very handsome – man he appeared to be; that sort never seemed to be alone, quite the opposite.

Walking past Nathan's room, I knocked loudly on the door. "This is your ten-minute warning, Nath," I called through the door. "I'm putting breakfast on and it's a treat, bacon and sausage."

I'd learned that a boy reaching his teenage years was better coaxed out of sleep, rather than having a short, sharp shock. I'd only tried that once and it hadn't ended well. Ben was right when he said surprises tended to result in an unexpected shift. I wouldn't ever try that method again; instead, I used the regular alerts, accompanied by the smell of breakfast being made.

Walking into the kitchen, I turned the grill on and then went to fill the kettle. The moment I turned towards the cupboards, my heart rate increased. There was a note propped against the kettle, the place Nathan knew was almost my first stop in the breakfast routine.

I knew what the note would say, yet there was little consolation in being right.

Sorry, Aunt Kerry, but I had to go with Ben. I need this. Please forgive my going against you, but I know he'll understand if the worst happens. Love you, Nathan xx

I could have stamped my foot in anger and frustration. I knew full well that Nathan needed to let off energy as his animal; I had done more research about being a shifter than I'd ever looked at anything else. I'd thought I'd convinced him with my findings and he was aware of how cautious he needed to be. I should have guessed that he didn't believe the true implications by the way he responded to Ben.

He'd been like a desperate boy, offered a lifeline. My anger faded as quickly as it had bubbled – he was as frightened and worried, if not more so, as I was. I should understand that he was going through these changes; if it was bad even for me, it must be ten times worse for him. He'd lost so much recently, I was wrong to try to stop him from having this one morning of freedom. I knew that Ben would look after him.

Turning to the kettle, there was nothing else for me to do but wait.

*

A few hours later, I heard a car swing into the parking area and rushed out to meet them. I had to know if it had gone wrong, that Nathan was still ok. Faltering at the open doorway, I realised too late that in my haste I had made a terrible mistake.

Stepping out of the car was the man and his cronies, whom I was desperate to avoid. How had they found me so soon? How could all my efforts these past weeks have been for nothing?

Terrified, but not about to go down without a fight, I stepped forward. At least Nathan wasn't here –

they could hurt me, but they wouldn't know where he was. That was the only positive in this utter mess.

"Well, isn't this a nice surprise?" Neil said, moving around to the front of the car, leaning on the bonnet and folding his arms, his smug smile making me grit my teeth.

"How did you find me?" There was no point beating around the bush; we'd been playing this cat-and-mouse game for too long.

"People in the right places and Nathan's phone," Neil said with a nonchalant shrug. "You should have checked Viv's phone – it was still linked to Nathan's. You're getting sloppy."

For the second time that morning, I could have growled in frustration. I hadn't thought to change Nathan's phone. No, I had thought about it, but presumed there was no need. He'd promised to play games on his phone without connecting to Wi-Fi; either my technology knowledge wasn't up to scratch, or he hadn't been sticking to his promise.

"He's not here." I shrugged.

Neil laughed, but there was no humour in it. "Of course he's not. You're just hiding here on your own. Don't treat me like a fool. Admit it – the chase is over. You tried to beat me, but Nathan is needed elsewhere."

"Is it that you're genuinely interested in Nathan, or that you can't let go that Viv chose me over you to be the guardian of her child?" I asked. I wasn't the sort of person who hated other human beings, but I detested this man as I'd never detested anyone else, and what made it worse was that he was related to me.

"I'm the head of the family," Neil said. It was always the same with him, his innate feeling of entitlement.

"This is not some sort of episode of *Downton Abbey*," I scoffed. I knew I was playing with fire. Neil didn't respond well to being mocked, but I thought it might give him pause to see me not worried that we were facing each other, when I usually tried to get away from him as quickly as possible. I just had to hope that Nathan and Ben wouldn't return yet, or my forced nonchalance would disappear in a second. "Being the eldest doesn't give you the right to interfere and offer up your nephew to the highest bidder."

"It's for the good of the shifter community."

I snorted. "Yeah, and there's no money headed your way at all." I knew my older brother far too well. He had few morals and even less family loyalty.

"He'll be well looked after."

"He'll be treated as a science experiment by the type of people who want to be able to reproduce who he is for their own gain."

"You're being too sentimental."

I shook my head at him in disgust and possibly hatred. "You just don't care that he's the only thing which links us back to Viv, do you? He looks like her, has the same mannerisms as her, and yet you're prepared to hand him over as you would anything which could bring you in more money."

"Viv isn't in a position to give a damn."

"No, but I do, and while there's breath in my body, you won't be able to get your hands on Nathan. I'm his guardian and you have no control over him. All I need to do is call the police and you'll be told to go away." I had tried this before, but all the police had said was that it would need to go through the civil courts if Neil was objecting to the guardianship. I couldn't afford a court case and Neil was fully aware of this.

"Interesting thought – if you were out of the way, the care of Nathan would revert to me."

"Are you threatening me?"

"I have witnesses who say not." Neil nodded to his ever-present posse of goons.

"Well just in case it was, you'd better know that if anything happens to me, there is someone already appointed to take over my role. You must consider me completely stupid if you didn't think I would make sure Nathan was safe, just as Viv made damn sure you couldn't touch him," I said.

Neil moved from his slouching position and stood, clearly intending to intimidate me, and to be honest, it was working. "You know I'm going to hound you until you give him to me, either willingly or not, don't you?"

"I've told you already, he's not here." I shrugged. "Let me guess – you've had some of your blood money up front and there are going to be angry people if you don't deliver him?" The betraying flush from Neil meant that I'd guessed right. Schooling my features into a bland expression, I folded my arms; I couldn't let him see that my assumption worried me even more, if that was at all possible. If Neil had already committed to delivering Nathan to the people who wanted to treat him as some lab rat, Neil would stop at nothing to get to him.

"You always were quick with your smart mouth," he growled at me. "Now you can stop with your comments if you know what's good for you and tell me where he is."

I opened my mouth to lie about what had happened to Nathan, but the sound of a vehicle approaching from behind Ben's lodge made me pause.

They were returning and walking into a situation which I couldn't warn them about. Even if Ben tried to help me by fighting with me against them if they tried to take Nathan by force, three against one weren't good odds, one and a half if I included myself. It wouldn't surprise me if Neil was armed either – it was the type of lowlife thing he would do, even when chasing his sister and nephew.

"Who the bloody hell is this?" Neil snapped. Just like every other bully, he didn't like an audience who wouldn't necessarily be on his side.

"It must be someone from one of the other lodges," I said with a shrug. "I think it's time you went, before I start to cause a scene."

"Just be careful what you do. There are a lot of roads which curl around the mountains and have very steep sides on either side in this area," Neil said. I could tell he was beginning to lose his patience and it wasn't looking good for me, but all I could do was mutter some inner chant, for Nathan not to come around the corner.

I closed my eyes in defeat when I heard Ben's cheerful voice, saying, "Morning, Kerry. Finally out of bed, are you?"

Chapter 5

Ben

Yawning as I locked my door, I turned when I heard a quiet movement behind me. I knew who it was, having already picked up his scent when I'd left my warm building.

"Morning, Nathan," I said quietly. I didn't think anyone was awake in the other lodges, but it was always a good thing to keep as quiet as possible.

"Am I still ok to come with you?" Nathan asked, his breath curling around him in the frosty air of the morning.

"What does Kerry say?"

"We had a long talk about it last night and she understands," Nathan said.

"Are you sure?" I wasn't convinced by his answer. Kerry had been adamant about not wishing Nathan to accompany me.

"She didn't want me to tell you about one part of my shifting. She worries that it will affect how people treat me, but I need to tell someone and get your advice, because it scares me," Nathan said.

He wasn't meeting my gaze, but at that moment, I didn't know whether or not it was because he was lying or that he was afraid to ask for help. I couldn't refuse the uncertainty in his voice. "Ok, let's get in the car, but I'm warning you – if I get into trouble from Kerry later, I won't be a happy tiger."

Nathan grinned. "I can't wait to see you change."

During the half-hour car journey, he chatted away until I reached the spot I always went to. It was secluded, away from the main parking spots, as there was no possibility of my leaving the car in a car park. I left my clothes in the car, so either returned to it naked or as a tiger, neither of which was advisable for anyone in the locality to see.

Nathan looked a little wary when I started to unbutton my shirt. "When you start to have to pay for your own clothing, you'll suddenly appreciate why shifters undress before they change. Clothing can hinder you if you need to change quickly, so it's best always to wear something which can be removed fast if needs be."

"I always seem to shift when I least expect it," Nathan admitted.

"With the exercises I taught you last night, you should soon start to be able to control your shifts a lot more. It's the same for everyone at the start." I noticed that he looked uncomfortable. "I'll get out of the car and let you change alone," I said, giving him some privacy.

Nathan stood on the opposite side of the car, shivering slightly. "Ben, this might not be what you expect…" he started.

"Do you want to shift first and then I'll follow when I know you're ok? Your animal will be fine with me. Don't worry if I give the occasional snarl; it is just my tiger asserting its authority. You are a young cub, so it won't hurt you," I said. Yesterday could have been a different scenario, but now that my animal knew about Nathan, there would be no threat from my beast.

"I hope I'm a cub," Nathan said quietly. He began to perform the motions that would initiate a shift. Seeming to struggle at first, he glanced at me in an appeal for help, but I just nodded in encouragement and remained watching. The brief smile on his face before he was covered in fur was something to behold, but it was nothing to the shock on my face when I realised what had happened.

A wolf was crouched in the place I'd expected to see a bear.

Whistling through my teeth, the wolf bounded around the car and snarled at me. "Easy, Nathan," I said soothingly. "Don't let your animal completely take over you. The two of you can co-exist. You know I'm your friend and not going to hurt you."

The wolf bowed its head slightly as if acknowledging what I'd said, and as I was freezing, standing naked in the cold, I decided that no matter what had happened, there wasn't time to dwell on it at this point if we wanted some freedom. With a mind racing through all sorts of scenarios, I shifted into my tiger form.

As predicated, my beast gnashed his teeth at the wolf, and Nathan bowed in submission. When the hierarchy was in place between the two animals, I led the way through the clump of trees we were parked beside. Turning back to ensure Nathan was following, I picked up speed after confirming that he was.

For the next hour, we ran across the snowy mountain tops, never stopping to admire the view, but just ploughing across the landscape, enjoying the feelings of freedom. At one point, I paused, breath billowing out in clouds, but my appreciation of the quiet was soon disturbed as the wolf launched himself at me and my tiger indulged the playful attack. We rolled and bounded around each other, paws batting, claws retracted so as not to inflict real harm.

Eventually, I led the way back to the car, both still running, but at a gentler pace than when we'd set out. As soon as we reached the car, I shifted, ready to assist Nathan, for I knew he would be exhausted. Panting at my side, he crouched and, after a slight delay, started to shift.

"That was awesome," Nathan said, before collapsing onto the ground. I quickly dressed and then scooped him up and put him in the car. It didn't matter that he was undressed; I put his seatbelt on and covered him with a throw. I'd expected this reaction – it took so much energy, he would probably sleep for hours with the amount of exercise he'd just had. I hadn't run at full speed; there was no way a wolf could have kept up with me, even a fully grown one, but he'd kept pace with the speed I'd set.

A wolf. It made sense why Kerry hadn't wanted Nathan to join me today. I'd heard about shifters who could change into different animals, but they were feared by many, even in the shifter community. It wasn't understood why it happened, and there was no group the shifter could belong to. None were welcoming to other breeds – to have one in their midst who could shift into anything would undermine the close-knit group.

Sighing, I glanced at the sleeping boy. It was a real shame, but he'd probably be an outsider for his whole life. I knew how that felt, but for different reasons. It was a lonely existence.

Wondering where they were headed and what his aunt's motives were as I drove back, I pulled into the parking space near my lodge. Opening my car door, I paused, sniffing the air a few times before pulling the door closed once more and turning to Nathan.

Shaking the boy roughly, I managed to wake him a little. "Nathan, this is important – wake up!" I hissed into his ear.

Moaning, he batted me away, but I persisted. Eventually, he blinked, trying to wake. "What is it?"

"Something's happening and I don't know what. Eat this," I instructed, handing him a bar of chocolate. "I want you to hide in the back of the car while I go and investigate." I'd picked up the scent of men, unfriendly men, and I'd also sensed Kerry's fear. I'd wanted to run out of the car and go straight to her side, but I was experienced enough to know that could cause more problems than it solved. I instinctively knew it had something to do with her desire to remain private and guessed it was because of Nathan, so my priority was to ensure he was safe.

My words had had the effect of bringing Nathan around a little; he looked afraid, but wolfed down the chocolate, knowing he might need the energy the sugar buzz could provide.

"Will you hide until I return from making sure it's safe for you to come out?" I asked. I was annoyed that the door to my lodge was visible from Kerry's lodge. I knew they were outside somewhere, and couldn't risk him being seen.

"It'll be Uncle Neil," Nathan said, with large, frightened eyes looking at me. "He's trying to take me away from Aunty Kerry."

"Ok, well, you can tell me all about Uncle Neil when I get rid of him." I knew Kerry could be doing something illegal with the child, but I had the feeling she wasn't. She cared about him too much, but I admitted I would have to keep my wits about me – a pretty face could be a criminal just as much as the cartoon images of criminals could be.

Nathan reached out and grabbed my arm. "He isn't nice. He'll hurt you if you try to stop him," he said.

"Is he a shifter?"

"No."

"Then I'd like to see him in a fight against my tiger," I grinned. I didn't normally promote violence, but I could see how afraid he was, and at the end of the day, he was a kid. If my words of bravado gave him a little courage while he waited, so be it.

It seemed they worked a little, as he smiled. "Your tiger is brilliant."

"Thanks. Now, you must promise to keep yourself safe until Kerry or I come for you. Understand?"

"Yes. Please don't let Uncle Neil hurt Aunty Kerry."

"That's an easy promise to make, pal," I said, getting out of the car. I quickly put on my jacket and slung a rucksack over my shoulder, as if I was coming back from a hike. Nathan had climbed into the footwell of the rear seats and had covered himself with the throw. It wasn't the perfect hiding place, but it would have to do for now.

Setting off around my lodge, I took in the scene as I approached the group. Three men faced Kerry, two remaining towards the back of the car, while one, presumably the feared Uncle Neil, stood in front of the vehicle. He'd definitely got two bodyguards from the size of them. They were standing, arms crossed across their chests, like they were out of some gangster movie. Bring it on, my tiger thought, and I had to agree with him as soon as I saw the expression in Kerry's eyes.

She was terrified but trying to cling on to a brave front. She'd looked at me in horror, but seeing her shoulders sag in relief, I knew her worry had been about Nathan. She pushed her glasses up her nose, an action I'd quickly begun to realise was her attempt to brace herself for whatever was coming. It was a nervous, but endearing gesture. A plan formed as I approached her, and it caused a smile to lighten my expression, which only increased when I saw puzzlement on Kerry's face.

"Morning, Kerry. Finally out of bed, are you?" I said, noticing that she closed her eyes in panic. Oh, she of little faith, I smiled inwardly.

Dropping my bag at my feet when I reached her, I wrapped my arm around her waist and pulled her towards me. Kissing her firmly, but briefly, I winked and smiled at her shocked expression, which she quickly covered. "Have I taken so long that you've decided to trade me in for a newer model?" I asked, nodding my head towards the three standing, all glowering at me.

"N-no, this is my brother," Kerry stammered.

"Ah, really? I kept my arm around Kerry's waist, but reached over to offer my free hand out for a handshake. "You must be Neil. I've heard a lot about you. Nice to meet you," I said easily, squeezing Kerry slightly in reassurance when she stiffened in my arms.

Neil reluctantly shook my hand, and I took some pleasure in the flinch he tried to hide, but failed to, when I squeezed his hand. Hard. "I've got business with my sister," he said, as if his words would have me scuttling away from them.

"I think you've finished here. What do you say?" I asked Kerry.

"I want them gone. There's nothing, or no one, they want here," Kerry said, glaring at her brother. "He's gone. You arrived too late."

"I don't think so," Neil said. "There hasn't been enough time, and his signal brought us straight here."

"Do you think I was going to risk being overtaken by you at some point?" Kerry snapped. "I gave us the start we needed, now Nathan isn't in my care anymore, and second by second he is farther away from you."

We heard the cry of a buzzard overhead, but I didn't betray the frown which threatened at the sound. I watched Neil as Kerry's words sank in.

"You stupid b—"

"I think you've said enough, and if you dare to insult *my mate* further, I might be forced to show you the error of your ways," I snarled. The emphasis on my wording was done purposely – only shifters used the term mate with regard to a partner. I was giving them a clear message, one which they'd obviously understood when the two bodyguards took a step forward. "I'd call your puppets off if I were you; you really don't want to make me angry." I allowed my tiger's anger to pulse off me, instead of restraining him as I usually did. They might not know what animal I was, but they were given a clear message that it was big and annoyed. Extremely annoyed.

"We'll find him no matter what you've tried to do to hide him," Neil sneered at his sister. He'd obviously decided that threatening me wasn't going to work. I wasn't weaker than they were, and let's be honest, bullies went after someone not as strong as themselves every time. "I'll never let this go."

"Nathan is protected and shall remain so until you call off the chase," I said. I didn't know all the details, but I knew enough.

"You might have the advantage now, but believe me, at some point you'll stop looking over your shoulder and I'll be ready." Neil spun on his heel and got in the driver's seat of the car, his two bodyguards climbing in the back, folding their bulk into the seats. As it screamed away from their parking spot, we stood and watched the car disappear.

"I-I-Nathan," Kerry started, seeming to slump into me.

Supporting her, I walked to my lodge. "He'll be fine. I think he's somewhere in the trees watching us, but I'm sure he'll join us soon."

"Trees? How did he get to the trees? I thought you'd walk around together..."

"I know. You must have been terrified. Here, sit down," I said, lowering her onto the chair next to the fire. I wrapped a throw around her; she was shivering. "I'll get the kettle on and then we can talk."

Filling the kettle, I went to the still-open door, and looking at the trees which reached the water's edge after the clearing in which the lodges were positioned, I whistled and held my hand up. I heard, rather than saw, the movement of feathers, and then the buzzard, which had flown by us, landed on my outstretched arm. Bringing it into the lodge and closing the door, I placed it on the sofa. Kerry watched my movements, wide-eyed.

"I think it's time to shift now before you collapse," I said to the buzzard. Within a second, Nathan's form changed back, and although he smiled at me in triumph, it was only a second before he slumped on the sofa unconscious.

"Is he ok?" Kerry immediately stood up, as always concerned for her nephew.

"He's absolutely shattered, but from the looks of it, very pleased with himself. Although when he wakes up, I'm going to make it clear in no uncertain terms that shifting when he was already weakened was foolish in the extreme. He could have fallen out of the tree he was hiding in," I said, moving back over to the kettle.

Making two hot chocolates and adding brandy to both, I handed one to Kerry. She took the cup from me. "He's never done that before," she said.

"Who? Neil or Nathan?" I sat opposite her.

"Nathan. He's never turned into a bird before. Neil has always been a selfish, arrogant, and nasty person. Nothing's changed there."

Smiling that she still had some fire in her, I took a sip of my drink, letting the smoothness warm my insides. "He has changed into different animals before, though, hasn't he? That was why you didn't want him coming out with me this morning, wasn't it?"

Closing her eyes for a moment, her shoulders slumped. "Yes."

"I'm not going to harm you or him in any way."

"It's hard to trust anyone when you can't even trust your own family," Kerry said bitterly.

"I think you should tell me everything, because whatever your plan is, I think you need my help. I don't think your brother is going to drive off and give up so easily – he didn't strike me as the kind."

"No. I would imagine he's going to be waiting at the end of the road until I leave. Nathan is too valuable to him for him just to let go, and he wouldn't have believed me when I tried to convince him that Nathan had gone to a place of safety."

"As Nathan needs hours of sleep, we can't risk going anywhere for now. Tell me everything."

Chapter 6

Kerry

Tell me everything. Three little words which frightened me and I longed for at the same time. It seemed a lifetime since I'd been able to trust anyone, and yet this stranger was asking me to put my faith in him that once he heard our story, he would disagree with Neil and not hand Nathan over as good as a sacrificial lamb.

When I'd seen him come around the corner, my knees had nearly given way, half through panic and half in relief that Nathan wasn't with him. The way he'd come to my side, protected me – no, almost staked a claim on me, had my hopes rising for the first time in a long time. Not of anything serious; I know his words and actions were intended to convey a message, but having someone there to offer support almost made me lightheaded with relief. Now I had to be honest, or I would lose his goodwill, and I wasn't in a position that I could afford for him to withdraw his help. I was being unfair – I wanted to be truthful, wanted to explain that my brusque behaviour was out of character, that I was a normal person underneath all this angst. That being in his arms had been the most comfort I'd received in a long time, but I couldn't say any of that. This wasn't about me and the way I'd reacted to him; it was about Nathan's safety.

"Nathan is my sister's boy, my baby sister. I'm the middle child, Neil being the eldest," I started. "Viv died a year ago in a car accident, and she left me as the sole guardian for Nathan."

"No, Dad around?" Ben asked.

"Unfortunately not." Kerry flushed. "He didn't even know Viv was pregnant. It was a short fling; he was passing through our town. She said they spent a fantastic week together and then he moved on. She never tried to get in touch with him when she found out she was pregnant. I've often wondered if having a child was her aim."

"A little unfair on the dad."

"Yes, it is, but Viv was similar to Neil in a way. They were both quite self-absorbed, although believe me when I say Viv was far more charming than Neil could ever be."

Ben smiled. "You don't like your brother much, do you?"

I couldn't help the laugh escaping as I put my empty cup down on the small table next to me. "No, I've never really liked him, but for what he's trying to do to Nathan, I despise him. I know it puts me in a terrible light, but not a day goes by without me questioning why Viv had to be taken when she loved Nathan, and we are left with Neil."

"Unfortunately, we don't have a choice in who we are related to," Ben said.

There was meaning in his words. I wondered about him. He seemed perfect on the outside – handsome, helpful, an all-round nice guy – but his words suggested that there was more to him than met the eye. I glanced around the lodge; it was very homely and cosy. It looked like the perfect hideaway, and from the little I knew about him, I suddenly wondered if he did indeed come up here to hide. The thought of him being lonely made my insides ache, but I pushed it aside. I couldn't dwell on a lonely tiger when I had Nathan to worry about. I smiled as my eyes rested on Nathan. He looked so young when he slept, his long eyelashes, which any girl would wish for, resting on his cheek as he breathed in his deep slumber.

"Are none of you shifters?" Ben asked, bringing my attention back to him.

"No."

"Then I'm presuming Nathan's father was?"

"Yes. I never met him, but Viv said he was. We didn't know whether Nathan was or not. In fact, we were beginning to think he wasn't, but just short of a year before Viv died, he changed for the first time."

"That must have been a bit of a surprise," Ben said.

"Sunday dinner at Viv's had never been so exciting." I smiled at the memory. "It was a shame – she refused to make cheesecake after that time, saying it brought back bad memories. She made a fantastic cheesecake, but Nathan splattered it across the room. Afterwards, I thought it was funny, but we hadn't a clue as to what to do at the time. We spent ages just trying to keep our distance, keep Nathan inside and talk him down until he shifted again."

"When did you find out he – for want of a better phrase – wasn't a normal shifter? Whatever that is," Ben asked. I appreciated the derision in his tone, knowing instinctively he wasn't being derisive about Nathan.

"We'd started to read and speak to people about how best to help Nathan in his transformation, and it went well until the third time he shifted, when he didn't shift into a wolf as he had done the first two times, but the bear you met yesterday," I explained. "The shifters in our town didn't react well to the fact, especially as the shift had occurred in one of Nathan's lessons with other young shifters."

"A wolf pack, at a guess?" Ben asked.

Nodding, I groaned. "Yes. The alpha had agreed to take Nathan under their wing and guide him. Needless to say, that arrangement came to an abrupt end on that third shift."

"They could have still helped him, but bloody wolves are a law unto themselves," Ben said.

"There was certainly no forgiveness when Nathan had erred in their eyes," I admitted. "We didn't know who to turn to for help, but then Neil got involved. He said he'd found a place, an organisation that wanted to work with Nathan. Viv thought it was a great thing at first, but thankfully, she insisted on finding out more rather than just blindly trusting Neil. It was essentially a science laboratory that sought to learn more about shifters, particularly those like Nathan. Apparently, they are rare."

"I've never met one before now, although I knew they existed," Ben said. "But I have heard of places that are unethical about research on the supernaturals of this world."

"I don't know how they can get away with it," I said. "Viv went absolutely ballistic at Neil, throwing him out of her house and telling him never to darken her door again. I think the day after that, she changed her will, so I would have responsibility for Nathan if anything happened to her."

"Do you think –" Ben said, but stopped when I nodded in agreement.

"Every day since the accident, I've thought that it didn't add up. It was too convenient," I admitted aloud for the first time. "The weather wasn't bad, Viv wasn't a speed freak, there was no oil on the road. They just said she lost control of the vehicle, but it was on a part of the road with no CCTV." I knew in my heart that Neil had somehow had something to do with Viv's death, but I would never be able to prove it and he was hardly likely to admit to it.

"I'm sorry. I've taken a career break from the police force, and I know what it's like when a case doesn't feel right. The gut instinct is rarely wrong," Ben said.

I let out a breath and looked at him. He was unwavering in his concern and sympathy, those amber eyes looking at me as if he could see into my soul. "If I'd known you were a police officer yesterday, you wouldn't have got into my lodge; they aren't my favourite people at the moment."

"Let me guess – you went to them about Neil and they advised you to go through the civil court?" Ben asked.

"Yes. So, not only did they not figure out that Viv's death wasn't an accident, about which I did admit my concerns to them, they didn't protect Nathan when he needed it."

"Or you," Ben said quietly.

"I'm irrelevant. Nathan's safety is all that's important."

"I beg to differ. You are both important," Ben said forcefully. "Don't forget yourself in all this."

How could so few words warm my insides so much? It had been so long since I'd received any affection from another human being – who wasn't Nathan, of course – that it made tears spring to my eyes. I blinked them away quickly. I had to stay strong; Neil couldn't win at this point. "I'll worry about myself when I know Nathan is safe."

"You've clearly got a plan. What is it? I understand if you don't want to confide in me, but I promise you I only want to help."

"I know you do and thank you, I appreciate it," I admitted. "I've arranged for him to be with those who are the same as him. I've found a community. They were hard to find, but one of the wolves gave me a hint about this group and I didn't stop until I'd found them. I've been in touch with their council, and they've said they'll welcome him and offer protection." It had taken months to find them and then a lot of hard work and persuasion for them to believe what I was saying.

"I didn't know there were enough of that type of shifter to make a community," Ben admitted. "Funny what you don't know about even with your own species."

"Apparently, they'll be able to teach Nathan how to control his shifts but embrace who he is," I explained. "If it weren't for Neil, he'd probably be able to leave them in a year or two if he wanted to. Unfortunately, while my brother is about, that won't be possible. He'll be stuck there."

"Where is it? Again, I understand if you don't want to tell me," Ben said.

"I have no choice." I smiled at him to take any sting out of the words. "I'm not foolish enough to try to reach the haven without your help. It's an island off the mainland. Stroma. Have you ever heard of it?" I asked.

"No," Ben replied.

"It's known as uninhabited; it suits the population who live on the island. They took some convincing that I was genuine, but there are people on the mainland who act as their go-betweens. It was like something out of a Dick Barton or James Bond book to set up meetings and persuade them to take Nathan on," I explained.

"You're too young to know Dick Barton," Ben said, and I laughed.

"It was my dad – he was into all the secret spy stuff. I've watched more black and white films than I care to remember."

"And what happens when you get there?"

"We stay until Nathan is settled in and then I have to leave." I had explained to Nathan what had to happen to keep him safe, and we'd both cried on more than one occasion. It would break my heart to leave him behind, but it was best for him. I knew that in the long term it was what he needed, but that didn't mean it hurt any less.

Ben watched me, as always, seeming to study me, before speaking. "How are you going to cope with leaving him?" he asked gently.

Once more blinking rapidly, I smiled. "By denying the reality of the situation until I'm forced to."

"You might not be safe when you come back to the mainland," Ben said.

"I'm not concerned about that," I admitted. "I know Neil is a nasty piece of work, but I don't care what he does to me as long as I've got Nathan to safety. I've been assured that enough wards and spells are protecting the island that no one gets access unless they are given the all-clear."

"You might not care about what happens to you, but I do," Ben said. He stood and started to pace across the room. "I'm not going to stand around while you sacrifice yourself to goodness knows what at the hands of your brother. When do you want to leave here?"

Although his words had filled my insides with warmth and even hope, his last question brought me back down to earth. "I don't know. We are booked into the lodge until tomorrow morning." Ben cocked an eyebrow at me at my admission that I'd lied yesterday when I said that we'd be leaving today, but although I flushed with guilt, I didn't apologise. I hadn't known he was such a good guy then. "Do you think I should leave tomorrow?" I wasn't one who would stand by and let someone else sort out my problems for me, or I wouldn't have got so far, but it was good to be able to speak to someone I'd very quickly come to trust.

"Staying here, we are just sitting ducks. What are your arrangements?"

"The boat will collect us from Gill's Bay tomorrow evening at four o'clock," I answered.

"Are you sure about them?" Ben asked. I knew why he was questioning me; it had sounded dodgy at first to me.

"As sure as I can be," I admitted.

"Ok. At the moment, Neil doesn't know which direction you are travelling in, so I change my mind on what I've just said. We will stay here. I'll shift this evening and sleep between the bedrooms. No one will get in, but I want to arrange a couple of surprises if I have your permission to speak to someone else about this?"

Unconsciously wrapping my arms around my middle, I shook my head in the negative. "No. I can't risk anyone else knowing anything."

Ben came and crouched beside the chair. Reaching out his hand, he grasped one of mine and pulled it to him, rubbing warmth into it. "I would trust Eddie with my life. As a tiger, he's fearless; as a human, he's the most withdrawn a person can be without being officially a hermit, but he is the best at – let's just say – making computers sing to his tune."

"How will that help us?"

"Think of most of the country covered in a network of computers – yes, all owned by different companies, but that doesn't stop Eddie," Ben said, pride and amusement in his eyes. "He's definitely a good one to have onside."

"You're a policeman and you are condoning hacking into systems," I said.

"I'm on a career break and I would never support the hacking of computers for financial gain or anything unethical, but if it means certain roads get closed, or particular cars are diverted from the way we want to go, then I don't have a problem," Ben said. He was grinning with devilment and I couldn't prevent the smile touching my own lips.

"He could do that?"

"Yes. And all from his cosy house in Bath," Ben said.

"Is he really trustworthy?" It was tempting to believe Ben, but what if his friend let us down? Including someone else was just giving me something else to worry about, and my nerves were already shot.

"Totally. It will make our journey easier," Ben said.

"Ok, talk to him."

Ben kissed the top of my forehead as he stood up. "You won't regret it."

No, I probably wouldn't, just like I didn't regret meeting Ben, and part of it had nothing to do with relying on him with regard to Nathan's safety. No. This had everything to do with me.

Chapter 7

Ben

I was playing with fire, being so forward with her, but every time she looked vulnerable and unsure, all I wanted to do was wrap her in my arms, kiss her and find ways to make her laugh. She didn't smile nearly enough, the worry about Nathan weighing her down. She'd had too much to deal with since her sister had died, and I wanted to bring some sparkle to her eyes. When I got a fleeting glimpse of her smile or her eyes lit up, I knew I could spend a lifetime trying to make her smile.

My timing was appalling. Of all the times to meet someone whom I could consider something long-lasting, we had to be fleeing from an angry family member. That my tiger didn't care and wanted me to claim her as my mate wasn't making for a comfortable day.

Shaking my head at the bad timing, I took my phone out of my pocket and dialled Eddie's number.

"Hey, Ben," the quiet voice of Eddie answered on the second ring.

"Hello, Ed. Fancy having a bit of excitement? From a distance, obviously," I asked.

"Thought you were after some chilling out time," Eddie said. "Been dragged into taking something on early? Charlie never mentioned anything about it."

"No. I've not spoken to Charlie for a couple of days. Someone is staying in one of the lodges who we need to help." I briefly explained what had gone on and smiled when I heard the whistle at the other end of the line.

"How do you find these situations? A mad witch-vampire, intent on destroying large parts of the supernatural world and then battling it out with goblins and warlocks. Anyone would think you revelled in this sort of thing," Eddie said of my last two significant cases while still working for the police. "What are we going to be facing going into partnership with you?"

"Too late to change your mind now. You've signed on the dotted line," I said of our new venture.

"Blast it," Eddie said. There was nothing but amusement in his voice. "What time are you setting off in the morning?"

"I'll say five; hopefully then there'll be fewer people on the roads, which I know will make us stand out for anyone wishing to follow us, but I have faith in you," I said.

"Don't worry, they'll have more to worry about than chasing you," Eddie assured me. "Give me the description of the car."

"It's a Mercedes saloon, registration GU68 NZS, black."

"Why do the criminally insane always choose black cars?" Eddie sighed. "They're so predictable."

"He's certainly criminal, but I'm not sure about the insane part," I laughed.

"He will be when you get away from him. Do you need any extra protection tonight?"

"No thanks. I'm going to shift and remain on guard. They don't consider me a real threat. There are three of them after all, and they'll arrogantly presume three against one is unbeatable. I've got a feeling they're on the main route, waiting for us to make a move. It's easier for an ambush to take place when we are en route, rather than trying to break in with the other lodges surrounding us."

"True, but just be careful," Eddie cautioned.

"I will be. See you soon. I'll send a text when we're setting off."

"Everything will be in place by then, don't worry."

"I've every faith in you. Bye."

Walking back into the central part of the room, I smiled at Kerry, who'd been watching my every move. "You're going to shift?" she asked, looking a little concerned.

"Yes. I'm amazing as a human, but I'm even more so as a tiger," I said, laughing at her eye roll.

For the rest of the morning and into the afternoon, we sat, chatting quietly while Nathan slept. We didn't discuss anything personal; we just talked about inane topics. I wanted her to relax, and it seemed to work as she snuggled into the seat. It was a strange situation, but the most content I'd felt in a long time.

Eventually, I roused myself; we needed an early night, so it was time to get organised. "Let's get ourselves a huge meal together. If we're moving off, I need to use up my supplies, and it might persuade Nathan to wake if he starts to smell food." The boy hadn't moved the whole time we'd been inside, still recovering from his exertions, but I knew that he would wake up ravenous.

"I have food in our cabin," Kerry said.

"Best we don't split up, and Nathan isn't ready to wake yet," I said. I hated that she immediately tensed at being reminded of the reality of our situation. "We're safe, Kerry, but we shouldn't underestimate them, or give them an opportunity to act. We'll get the food tomorrow before we leave."

"Tell me what you want me to do to help," she said, moving over to the kitchen area. "Doing something will stop me feeling so helpless."

I shot her a smile. "You aren't helpless. In fact, you remind me very much of a witch I know. She's capable and stands up to people, even when the odds are against her, just like you did with your brother and his goons."

"I was scared to death that you and Nathan would walk around the corner," Kerry said. "I nearly collapsed when I saw you alone and guessed you had seen something of what was going on."

"I'd not seen anything, but I'd picked up the scent as soon as I opened my car door," I responded.

"Could you smell us from that distance?"

"I knew there were strangers and I could tell they weren't of the friendly variety. I could also sense your fear," I said gently. "Although it didn't show on your face when I came around the corner."

"I wish I'd had that skill, then I wouldn't have gone barging out of the door when I heard a car arriving, thinking it was you two and ready to give Nathan a piece of my mind for going against my wishes."

"Ah, hell. I thought he might have sneaked out," I said. "I'm sorry. I should have checked with you that you had experienced a change of heart rather than taking the word of an excited kid."

"It's ok," Kerry said, starting to chop some chicken that I'd handed her into pieces. "I know he needs to be able to release some of the urges he has. I should have listened to you in the first place, but I suppose it doesn't matter now."

"It has shown that Nathan is even more talented than you thought. Turning into a bird after the exercise he'd undergone was no mean feat. He's going to be one powerful shifter within a very short space of time."

"As long as he's happy," Kerry said. Her voice was small and I knew she was thinking of when she would have to leave him on the island. "So, tell me about this witch. Is she someone special?"

Did I imagine the faint blush on her cheeks as she asked the question? I hope I hadn't imagined it, because if she was feeling only half of what I was, it was a good thing. "She is special, but as a friend. She's very much in love with a vampire."

"But if she was available?"

I laughed. "No, it would never work between us. She could never forgive me for having such perfect skin."

Kerry spluttered a laugh. "What?"

"The first time I met her, I thought she was in some way prejudiced against shifters, because she couldn't stop staring. When I challenged her over it, she admitted that she'd never seen a man with such smooth, unblemished skin. She wanted to know if I'd suffered from acne as a teen."

Grinning at me, Kerry raised her eyebrows. "And did you?"

"No. Shifters heal really well."

"That's so unfair!"

"You've just said the same words that Jenny did. I don't think she ever forgave me, although she did save my life recently, so perhaps she had."

"Really? How?"

"I'd been injured in a job and she gave me some of her life essence; it nearly killed her in the process. She hadn't known how it would affect her; she'd just acted when faced with my injuries," I explained briefly. The whole episode still gave me nightmares, especially about being so useless in a dangerous situation, plus what it had nearly cost Jenny.

"She sounds amazing," Kerry said.

"I think you'd get on with her," I said. "You've heard all about my dark and dismal past – what about you? What do you do for a living?"

"I work in a bank. Very boring, very predictable. I've taken some time off, though. I decided that it wasn't safe for me to be out of contact for eight hours a day when Neil was trying to sell Nathan off as a lab rat."

"Will you go back to it when Nathan's settled?"

"I'm not sure what I'll do. I was hoping to stay near him on the mainland, but I've Googled all around here and there aren't many large towns where I could disappear. If Neil can find me, it will put Nathan at risk, or even the whole island. I realise I could be used against Nathan as a bargaining tool, and I can't put Nathan or the island in that danger."

"I wouldn't worry about that too much. The fact that I've never heard of it means there's a good chance they've got this concealment lark off to a tee. Now, come on, you're slacking and I'm hungry."

Kerry huffed good-naturedly but sped up her chopping. Within the hour, we had a chicken and chorizo paella, salad and crusty bread all set out on the table. I opened a beer and Kerry accepted one, before we woke Nathan.

The food smells had obviously started to seep into his unconscious state, as he soon came round at our coaxing. His stomach growled with hunger as he opened his eyes and he grinned. "That smells good."

"There's plenty of it. Come on, tuck in," I said. I'd been the one staying near him while waking him. I didn't want to be unable to react if he was startled enough to shift, but it seemed there were no adverse effects from waking him early.

We sat around the table, and there was no problem with worrying about what we were going to speak about – Nathan bombarded me with questions throughout the meal, to the point when Kerry held up her hands to stop the flow.

"Nathan! Enough! Ben's hardly had time to eat, while you've asked question after question and been shovelling food while he's answered," she said.

"But I'm hungry and want to know everything," Nathan said, reaching over to the bowls in the centre of the table to load his plate up for the third time.

"It's ok, I'll be testing him on my answers later," I responded.

Nathan's hand stilled in mid-air. "Will you?"

"No, but I'm highly insulted that you haven't absorbed everything I've said." I shook my head at Nathan in amusement. I'd have loved to be able to ask the questions at the start of my own shifting experience, which he was asking now – they were the natural whys and hows of any shifter learning about his skill.

"It's a lot to take in, isn't it?" he said with a grin, happily piling food on his plate. It was a good thing we'd used up all my fresh food; his appetite seemed never-ending, but to be fair, he had expended a lot of energy.

"It is, but you'll have support when you get to the island," I assured him. "I'm just jealous of your ability and slightly annoyed that you didn't listen to my instructions. I should tell you off, but I'm more curious to know why you decided to do what you did."

"I was going to wait," he admitted with the honesty only a young child can offer. "But then I thought, what if they came around the corner, or if they had someone hiding nearby? I was going to sneak into your lodge, but didn't for the same reasons. I knew if I changed into any animal, they'd know immediately that it was me and chase me. I sat there and thought if only I could fly, I'd be safe, and then it struck me. Perhaps I could fly."

"What animals have you changed into before now?" I asked.

"We thought he was a wolf at the start," Kerry said. "As I said earlier, it was a wolf cub, wasn't it, little wolf?"

Nathan smiled at her before looking at me seriously. "Yes, but then one day I was messing around with my best friend, who was also a wolf, and he hurt me as we were play-fighting. I stood up to shout at him, and the next thing I knew, I was a bear."

"That must have been a shock for both of you," I said.

"I thought something had gone very wrong with me, and it caused all sorts of trouble with the wolf pack, didn't it, Aunty Kerry?"

"It certainly did," Kerry said. "There were so many trips to the doctors, but they were as baffled as we were. The wolves didn't want anything to do with him, and then Neil started coming around. The rest you know about."

"You'll be settled soon, pal," I said to Nathan. "It's a great talent you have – don't ever forget that."

We cleared up the lodge and I looked at the clock. "Set your alarm for four. We can spend an hour loading the car up and then set off at five. Will an hour be enough to pack?" I asked Kerry.

"Yes. I haven't really unpacked in case we had to leave quickly."

"Good. We'll take my car."

"Where should I leave mine?"

"In my parking space. I can always arrange for it to be transported somewhere for you when you know what's happening." She knew I meant when she was ready to leave Nathan; there was no need for me to utter the words and remind them both of their future separation. "I want to drive in case there is any need to lose someone on our tail."

"Is it going to be some sort of police chase?" Nathan asked eagerly.

"I hope not!" Kerry admonished him. "We want to reach the dock safely. Oh, one other thing. You are going to have to leave your phone here."

"Aw, why?" Nathan moaned.

"It's the way Uncle Neil found us," Kerry said.

"But it's got all my games on and my mates' numbers."

"Your friends can't know where you are," Kerry said quickly.

"I know that, but are you expecting me to just cut myself off from them completely?" Nathan demanded, the first time I'd seen him argue against anything that Kerry had said.

"You can't put the other islanders at risk," Kerry said gently. "They're offering you a safe place to go. You can't repay them by putting the whole community in danger."

Nathan looked as if his worries had returned at Kerry's words, and I could tell from her stance that she had regretted reminding him that they were at risk. "Come on, time for bed," I said. "I don't want any whinging when I get you up at four in the morning. Nathan, you're in the room on the left through the kitchen, and just so you know, I'm going to be in tiger form – I don't want you getting a nasty surprise if you decide to go to the bathroom in the night."

He grinned. "I won't. I'm still tired. Night," he said, taking himself off to bed.

"Tomorrow is going to be a long day," Kerry said. "I can sit up and listen out. I don't want you to be too tired to drive."

"I won't be, I promise. I can sleep while being on guard."

"But—"

"Have you never heard of cat-napping?" I couldn't help grinning at her exasperated look as she realised there wasn't anything she could say to change my mind.

"Good night," she said. "Thank you for this."

"You're welcome." I waited until she'd entered the second bedroom in the lodge and closed the door. Undressing quickly, I transformed into my beast and padded over to the hallway which separated the two bedrooms and bathroom. Flopping down on the floor, my tiger sighed and I completely understood why. He was convinced that Kerry was the perfect mate for me, and instead of being curled up with her, we were outside her door, able to take in her scent and doing nothing at all about it. It was going to be a long night.

Chapter 8

Kerry

I heard the tiger thud onto the floor as it, no, *he*, settled down for the night. I had never felt so drawn to a person I had only just met. It was crazy really; this whole situation was turning out completely different to what I'd expected. If I'd known who I would find here, I'm sure I would have rushed here months ago and begged him for help.

For the first time since Viv's death, I no longer felt out of my depth. Ok, I might still be in unchartered waters, but I didn't feel alone, and that was a relief, reassuring and comforting all mixed to create a heady mix. Add the fact that the person who was offering such support was an absolute hunk of a man, and I could go to sleep with a smile on my face. The only sticking point was that he was a tiger.

Oh, I wasn't prejudiced against shifters, or any other form of supernatural being; it was just that I had no experience of them, except to know that in a lot of cases, they stuck with their own kind. That was a depressing thought and had intruded into my thoughts all evening.

After Neil had been sent away, I was able to pretend for a few hours, mostly at least, that I belonged to a normal family. One who prepared meals together, who chatted around a table, who liked each other and had everyone's best interests at heart. It had been lovely, a snapshot of how life could be.

I doubted that I'd be able to sleep tonight; apprehension at what we would face tomorrow caused spikes of fear to pulse through me. Could Ben and his friend protect Nathan? I had no idea why they would go to so much trouble, but I was thankful for it.

Hearing a sigh outside the door, I climbed out of bed. It seemed someone else wasn't sleeping either. Opening the door slowly, I couldn't help the intake of breath when I saw the size of the beast that was lying across the hallway.

The stripes along his body rippled as he lifted his head at my appearance. Staring at each other, my expression probably revealed the nervousness I felt, while I was sure I could only detect curiosity in his.

"I couldn't sleep," I whispered, not wanting to wake Nathan but doubting I would. That boy could sleep with an earthquake going on around him.

Standing, the tiger took a few steps to reach me. I was still partially hidden behind the half-opened door, not quite sure of what to do. As I reached out with my hand, he knocked it so that his head was underneath.

Chuckling, I scratched his head, surprised at the depth of the fur. "You expect me to believe that you're just your common or garden house cat, do you?" I scratched his head anyway and had the pleasure of seeing him close his eyes in pleasure.

Being braver than I thought I was capable of, I moved from behind the door and into the hallway, sinking to my knees and sitting crossed-legged next to the tiger, continuing to rub his head, which now I had to reach up to do. He only paused for a second before lying down at my side, his body touching mine.

"I'm going to regret this in the morning when I'm worried about you driving and being alert," I admitted. He huffed and gave me a sideways glance, which made me smile. "You aren't two separate beings, are you? I can see Ben's expression in your glance. No, I'm not doubting your ability. I'm a born worrier, that's all."

He nudged my stomach, and at first I wondered what he wanted me to do, but with a few gentle pushes with his nose and curling his body around me, I worked out that he wanted me to lean against him. Even though he was shifted, I couldn't stop the blush tinging my cheeks as I did as he silently suggested. Although it was exquisite, like leaning against the most comfortable cushion ever.

Twisting so I could lean across his back while still scratching his head, I was able to relax a little. It was soothing, feeling his steady heartbeat and rhythmically stroking him. "I'm not sure what I'm going to do once I hand Nathan over to the others," I admitted. "I realise that sounds really selfish, but it's the truth. I'm beginning to realise that once Nathan is settled, I need to do something different, anything as long as it's far away from my blasted brother and his cronies. I've never travelled. Perhaps I need to book a one-way ticket for an around-the-world trip."

The tiger grumbled low in his throat, at which I chuckled. "What's up? Don't think I'd manage on my own? I'd certainly make some mistakes, that's for sure. I have done on this trip. Perhaps I'll spend the year on a beach. Yes, somewhere warm, with a blue, clear sea and no hassle. Perfect." My words received another growl. "Want to come with me?" I asked, feeling bolder as he wasn't in human form and I couldn't see his eyes from where I was sitting. I received a purr in response to my question, which made me laugh again. "It's a deal then. You can accompany me and I'll buy the drinks."

After another purr, we lapsed into silence. The night was quiet and still outside; there were no sounds to put me on my guard and I felt myself relaxing. Yawning, I promised myself I would only close my eyes for five minutes and then return to my bed – just five minutes of being snuggled up to a warm, furry beast.

*

"Aunty Kerry, what are you doing on the floor?" Nathan asked, as I blinked rapidly to try and work out what he was saying, where I was and what time it was.

"Urgh. What?" I sat up and only then realised I was lying beside Ben, still in tiger form, and I could swear that he was grinning at me. Jumping up, I tried to straighten my hair, but from the look on Nathan's face and the way Ben was stretching in a cat that got the cream sort of stretch – he seemed so pleased with himself – my hair was the least of my worries. "What time is it, Nathan?" I asked, trying to gain some control of the situation.

"I don't know, but your alarm was going off for ages."

Walking back into the bedroom, which I should have returned to before closing my eyes, I silently cursed to myself. My alarm had worn itself out and was on snooze. It must have been trilling for five minutes and I hadn't heard a thing. That sent a shiver down my back, thinking of what we could have missed while being asleep. Switching the alarm off, I returned to the hallway.

"It's ten past four and – oh my word...!" Ben had shifted while I'd been in the bedroom. All six feet plus of athletic build stood before me, absolutely naked. "Oh – I..."

"Sorry, I thought you were going to use the shower," Ben explained with an unembarrassed grin. "Mind if I grab a quick one while you're gathering yourself?"

"I – er, yes, of course," I stuttered. Keep the eyes on his face, keep looking at his face, I chanted silently to myself.

Ben turned to Nathan. "I have some steak in the fridge for our breakfast. Do you think you could shift into wolf form without leaving the lodge? It could be a stressful day, and shifting now will take the edge off your urges whilst we're driving," he explained.

"Are there going to be car chases?" Nathan asked, totally unfazed by Ben's state of undress.

"I hope not, but there's always the possibility," Ben said. "Now stop wasting time. Shift."

Nathan didn't argue further, but shifted into wolf form as requested. I was so impressed that he'd been able to control which animal he changed into that I'd forgotten about Ben for the moment.

"I shan't be long and then I'll get breakfast on while you get ready," Ben said. I turned back to him and looked down before catching myself. I met his gaze; he was chuckling at my flushed cheeks. Winking at me with a grin on his face, he left me in the hallway, blushing like a schoolgirl.

Nathan's long snout nudged me, which stirred me into action. I picked up his discarded clothes. I could hear the shower, but hurried into the kitchen before the water stopped. I might not have minded at all if I got a glimpse of that fine body again, but we had a task to do, and that was the most important thing for today.

Walking into the kitchen, I put the kettle on. Nothing set me up like a good cup of tea. Thankfully, it looked like Ben was a tea fan, as there was a big box of tea in his cupboard. I popped some bread in the toaster and sorted myself out. I would have started on Nathan and Ben's breakfast, but I had the idea what having steak meant – I didn't think it would involve using the cooker, and to be honest, it was way too early in the morning for me to start dealing with raw steak.

Ben walked out of the bedrooms, a rucksack over his shoulder and a suitcase in his hand. "That was quick," I said.

"I've trained myself to be very efficient at packing and unpacking over the years," Ben said. "Shower's free if you want to have one, while I feed the hungry wolf here."

Nathan had been walking around the lodge, using the time to sniff and explore the areas he wouldn't in human form.

"Thanks. I won't be long," I said, leaving Ben and Nathan to it.

Returning to the kitchen fifteen minutes later, I had a small towel wrapped around my hair. Ben looked at me and smiled. "Ah, sorry, no hairdryer."

"It's ok. When we're ready to go, I'll blast mine from our lodge. Nathan, you'd best shift now." He was busy licking the bowl, which had been on the floor. He'd obviously enjoyed his breakfast.

Nathan looked to Ben, and on his nod he started to shift. Within a moment, he stood before us, not collapsing as he usually did.

"It seems like a controlled shift doesn't tire you as much as normal," I said to him.

"It's been for a short time and he's eaten whilst shifted, which gives him energy," Ben explained. "Come on, Nathan, time to get a move on."

Without uttering a complaint, Nathan went towards the bathroom. "I need to have a little of your power," I said. "One word from you and he does exactly as you say."

"It's purely the novelty of having someone who is similar, for once. I'm sure it would soon wear off if I was around for a long time," Ben said. I knew his words weren't right; he'd offered Nathan so much already, showing him what he needed to do, tricks of the trade almost, it was natural that Nathan would respond so positively to him. I couldn't see that wearing off.

It wasn't long before we were waiting at the door, ready to leave. Ben looked at us both. "There's no one near the lodges, but just as a precaution, we are going to stick close together. Go straight to your lodge, gather what we need as quickly as possible, and then come directly to my car. I'm going to contact Eddie now and he will set things in motion. All being well, by the end of today we'll be on that boat over to Stroma."

We nodded our agreement and the three of us left Ben's lodge. I trusted Ben; I trusted everything that he said, but it didn't stop my heart pounding in my chest as we covered the short space between the two lodges. At any moment, I expected to hear Neil's voice through the night air, but thankfully, there was just the silence and peace of a world still asleep.

The lodge was freezing, as the heating had not been on overnight. It helped to spur us into grabbing all our luggage as quickly as possible, and within twenty minutes, it was as if we'd never actually been there; all was in order. Gathering once again on the inside of a lodge doorway, Ben smiled at us in reassurance.

"The next part is going to be ok," he said confidently. "Although there might be moments when it doesn't feel that way. I've sent a text to Eddie and he is arranging a little diversion for us. Don't be alarmed when you see a police car, possibly with flashing lights. Nathan, I'm counting on you to stay calm and utilise some of the exercises I've taught you. I don't want to be worried about you shifting while we are driving and then your animal reacting badly to being confined in a seat belt."

"I promise I won't shift," Nathan said. It was the first time he had sounded really confident and in control about anything to do with him being a shifter, and even though it had only been less than two days, the change was marked.

Ben took hold of my hand and squeezed it in reassurance before he opened the door, and the three of us moved as one, all struggling with our luggage but being as quiet as we could be.

We reached Ben's car without incident, and I released a breath when we were inside and Ben locked the doors. He glanced at Nathan in the rear-view mirror and shot a glance in my direction. Smiling at us both, he said one word. "Ready?" We both nodded and he started the car.

Chapter 9

Ben

Wanting to dwell on the fact of having Kerry curled against me for hours last night was unfortunate in the circumstances I was facing at the moment. I couldn't afford to let my mind wander. Plus, I would've loved to rejoice in the fact that she was relaxed enough with me to go to sleep by my side. It had sent a sensation through me which I'd never experienced before. It wasn't the urge to protect; I felt that every day in my job as a police officer. It was more than that – almost an overwhelming need to care for her, to make her life better in any way I could.

My tiger was almost rolling his eyes in exasperation at my not making the move I could have done last night. Still, I am gentleman enough not to take advantage of a woman in a vulnerable situation. Even though that caused numerous rumbles of discontent from my tiger, that's the downside of having a beast as your animal. His natural urges wouldn't necessarily understand, but he was astute enough to know that no matter how hard he tried to push and persuade me, my standards would never alter.

As soon as I set off in the car with my two passengers, I phoned Eddie. His voice came over the in-car speaker system as clear and awake as if it wasn't five o'clock in the morning and he hadn't been up all night, which I was sure a lot of the nights he was. There was no other explanation as to why he was always contactable.

"Morning, Ben," he started, as calm as ever. "Everything is in place. The police should be arriving just about now."

"Where is the vehicle?" I asked.

"At the junction with the main dual carriageway. There wasn't really any other spot they could have chosen. They've not moved all night, so I would imagine they are hungry, tired and grumpy by now. The perfect time to be greeted by the local police force."

I laughed. "You have a wicked streak in you, Eddie," I said. "That quiet demeanour you portray is only a façade, isn't it, pal?"

"Not at all," Eddie replied, but there was a laugh in his voice.

"We're approaching the end of the road now," I said, becoming serious once more. "Kerry, Nathan, can you please crouch down in your seats? I know it will be uncomfortable, but I would rather it seem that I'm alone for the police to see at least. I realise it won't fool Neil, but I'd rather him not be able to see you as we pass."

"Why aren't you driving faster?" Nathan asked, but he was doing as I had instructed.

I could tell by his tone that he was worried and afraid. "Nathan, if I race past this police car, he will be obliged to chase me, no matter what reason brought him to your uncle's car. Don't worry, I will be putting my foot down the moment we have moved out of sight. Keep doing those breathing exercises. Don't worry, you can keep hold of your control. Just remember, you are the human and your animal will do whatever you command it to." The rumble in my chest suggested that my animal disagreed with my comment, but for now, it would have to be angry with me, as I needed to keep Nathan calm and reassured.

"You're just about to pass the police car now." Eddie's voice came over the line, focusing us all.

The air in the car stilled as we all held our breath as we passed the Mercedes. The police car was parked across the front of Neil's car, which would prevent him from making a hasty escape if he tried. It would give us an extra few seconds when the police decided that Neil and his cronies were, in fact, not doing anything wrong as far as they were concerned.

Turning onto the main road, I turned to Nathan, quickly glancing at him. "You can both get up now," I said. "How are you feeling, Nathan?"

"I'm ok," he replied, but I could see the strain on his face.

"Just concentrate, pal. We're on our way now." They both settled in their seats and I pressed my foot harder on the accelerator. "What's next, Eddie?" I asked.

"Take the third turn off and then follow that road all the way through the Cairngorms," Eddie replied.

"You're taking us through the mountains?" I asked. The road might be more direct, but it wasn't straight, and with snow on the tops, it would be harder to drive through.

"Yes, and hopefully if you get there before they realise which route you've taken, they won't be able to trace you because the snow gates will have closed behind you."

"You can do that?" Kerry asked, speaking to Eddie for the first time.

"Yes. It's extremely easy when you know how," Eddie replied.

I could see the wheels of Kerry's mind ticking over as she weighed up the implications of Eddie being able to control something that was owned by the council or highways.

"Don't worry," I said, interrupting her musings. "We aren't a gang of criminals, I promise you."

She smiled a little, but I could appreciate that she was no fool, and the more she saw of what Eddie could do, the less she would trust us. We were flying close to what was legal and not, but it would take too long to try and explain the ins and outs of how we'd set things up. When it came down to it, I didn't care what we did as long as Nathan and Kerry were safe at the end of the day. For the first time in my life, I didn't care whether we acted criminally or not.

Eddie's voice interrupted my musings. "They've left their position now," he said. "The police car departed two minutes ago and the Mercedes is following in your direction. I'd put my foot down a little more if I were you, Ben."

I did as he said and the car lurched forward. I was thankful we had a steady 4x4 at our disposal. Visiting often during the winter months, the car was perfect for coping with the roads of the Cairngorms. I turned off the road as Eddie had instructed, but a sharp intake of breath at the other end of the phone made me realise that the Mercedes was gaining ground.

"How far is it to the first snow gate?" I asked.

"About a mile. I could really do with a bit of distance between you and them," Eddie said. "The gates are responsive, but they do need a few seconds to close."

"I hear you, Ed, and I'm trying my best," I said, pressing harder on the accelerator pedal. I knew Kerry was holding onto the side of the seat, but I couldn't afford to take my eyes off the road to reassure her with a glance or a smile. The road wasn't a twisted and turning country road by any means, but there were bends and dips that, at the speed I was travelling, required my full concentration. Nathan was noticeably quiet, and again I just hoped that he was practising his relaxation techniques, because I could see the black Mercedes in my rear mirror and I agreed with Eddie – there wasn't enough distance between us both.

My car shot past the first snow gate, and all credit to Eddie, he'd already started closing it, but there was plenty of room for me to get through as I travelled along the centre of the road. I wasn't sure whether this would be the barrier that would stop the Mercedes, so I didn't let up on the speed.

"Dammit," Eddie said, giving me the update that I hadn't wanted. The Mercedes had got through the barrier. "On the next gate, I need more distance between both cars, Ben. You've got to go faster."

"When is the next one?" I asked.

"Two miles. Come on, Ben, you're going to have to put your foot down."

"I am not about to get us all killed, but I promise you I'm going as fast as I can," I answered. The car was suited for heavy going over snow and rough terrain, but needing to fly almost at the speed of light across roads, as was required now, was not what it was made for. I was making the engine scream in my attempts to put some distance between us.

Unfortunately, the sleek lines of the Mercedes were keeping up with me. Kerry twisted in her seat and looked back through the rear window before turning to me in horror. "They're gaining on us," she said in a whisper.

"I don't want to risk us crashing," I ground out with teeth gritted as I concentrated on pushing the car further forward.

"Ben, drive faster!" she shouted at me.

Surprised at the forcefulness in her voice, I instinctively pressed my foot as hard as I could. The accelerator pedal was now as flat on the car interior as it could be; it literally couldn't go any further. If this didn't give us the gap we needed, nothing would.

We almost flew past the next set of gates, which had closed more than the first set had. I breathed in when we passed them as if it would help make us fit.

"Are they getting through the gates?" I asked Kerry.

She glanced behind us again and sucked in a breath. "Yes," she said. "Something flew off the car as they passed it. I think they struck the gate, but they are still behind us." She turned to Nathan on hearing a sound behind her, speaking firmly to him. "Nathan, you have to concentrate. Don't look back, don't think about what's happening; breathe, as Ben taught you, and stay in human form. Can you understand how important this is?"

I didn't hear an answer from Nathan, so I presumed he'd just nodded when Kerry turned and faced forward once more. I could sense that she was terrified, but I knew without a doubt that it was the terror of being caught by her brother, rather than anything we were doing.

"One mile the next one, Ben," Eddie's voice came over the speakers. "This might be a tight squeeze, Ben, but don't let up on the speed. Keep going, just keep going," he urged me.

"Got it," I ground out. My jaw was hurting from gritting my teeth at the need to hold my nerve. I heard the barrier scrape along the side of the 4x4 as we passed it and winced at the fact that my pride and joy would probably have great gouges down each side when we eventually stopped, but I kept going, not letting up on the speed.

"They've stopped," Eddie said. "The barrier is shut completely."

Kerry swung round to look behind "They have," she said in relief.

"I half expected them to crash through it," Eddie said. "But hopefully this is giving you a head start that will make all the difference. They will know which road you are coming out of, as this is the only main passable road over the mountains, but this is giving you a mighty good start. You need to keep the pressure on to make sure the distance between you both is maintained. Keep that bloody foot on that pedal."

I smiled at Eddie's words. That was cursing indeed from my mild-mannered friend. "Thanks, Ed," I said, hoping my two words conveyed the genuine gratitude I felt. We wouldn't have got this far without Eddie's help.

"I'll leave you to it for now," Eddie said. "But I'll monitor your progress and that of the Mercedes. If there's anything to report, I will let you know as soon as anything changes."

"Thank you. Bye," I responded.

Silence reigned in the car for a little while as I kept the speed up as fast as I could, although admittedly, my foot was no longer pressed firmly on the floor of the car, as I didn't think we needed quite that much speed. We were at less risk of losing control at our marginally slower speed.

After a few moments, I risked a glance over my shoulder. "You ok, Nathan?" I asked.

"Yes, thanks," Nathan said, but his voice was strained, and I could tell the stress of the journey was taking a toll on him.

"Why don't you try and close your eyes?" I suggested. "I know it's a bumpy drive, but you'll be tired from all that has gone on this morning, and eventually we'll reach a bigger road and it'll be a smoother drive. If you do manage to get to sleep, I've got a large bar of chocolate in the glove compartment for when you wake up."

"That sounds good," Nathan said. "I will try to sleep. I'm exhausted."

"Are you trying to get my nephew completely addicted to sugar?" Kerry asked.

I sent her a smile. "You wouldn't believe how much energy we use up in a day. Don't worry too much about his calorie intake."

"I tried to research as much as I could about shifters once we realised what was happening with Nathan," Kerry admitted. "It seems there is so much more that I need to learn."

"It's one of those things that, unless you are in the middle of it, there's always something else to take up your time, and that stops you getting all the information you need to be fully informed," I assured her. "Plus, when you think about it, I should know a lot more about Nathan's situation than I do, being a shifter myself. It's amazing what he can do and what he will be able to do with further training. I am quite envious."

"How does it feel when it first starts?"

"It's strange and confusing and a little bit scary, even though you've been expecting it," I admitted. "Quite often there are surprises along the way that nobody could have foreseen." Especially in my situation, I mused to myself. My words were a hint about my past, more than I'd said to anybody else.

"There certainly was in Nathan's case," Kerry acknowledged. "It sounds like you haven't had an easy time of it either."

"You could say that," I replied, but that was as far as I was prepared to go into what my experience of being a shifter was. I didn't mind helping Nathan, but going back into my own history couldn't cause anything but angst and upset, and now wasn't the time. I was beginning to get the distinct impression that Kerry was interested in me, and I really wanted to try to encourage her, but our timing was far from perfect.

"It's beautiful here," Kerry said, glancing out of the window.

I smiled. "I'm surprised you can take it in at the speed we're going."

"Yes, it is a bit of a rally race and not the perfect way to travel through the mountains, but even the speed we're going at can't prevent me from being awed by the beauty of the place."

"I love it here," I admitted. "But part of that affection is the remoteness, the lack of people and the ability to run free. I have a friend, Charlie, and he keeps trying to persuade me to move to the States and set up our business there so that I can truly appreciate the wide open spaces over there."

Kerry's head swung to look at me. "You're not going, are you?"

"Would you miss me?" I asked.

The atmosphere changed in the car and it was a few moments before she replied. "Yes, I would," she answered quietly.

"In that case, I'm not going."

"Good," she said, pushing her glasses up her nose.

*

As soon as we reached the other side of the mountains, Eddie rang once more. "The problem with Scotland is that there aren't a huge number of roads," Eddie said as a greeting.

"How far behind us are they?" I asked.

"Far enough for the moment. I'm guessing they might already have a suspicion that you're trying to leave the mainland," Eddie said.

"As long as the boat comes as arranged, we should be able to get away before they reach us. I'm hoping that the island will have enough protection on it that we'll disappear off the radar," I said.

"That would prove useful at this point," Eddie responded. He paused, and I could almost hear the cogs turning as he watched a screen or monitored some device within his arsenal.

"What is it, Eddie?" I asked, immediately alert to the fact that something was bothering him.

"They've just passed a junction, one where the right-hand lane would have taken them to a larger town and harbour than the one you're heading for, but they took the left-hand lane. Almost as if they know which direction you're going in," Eddie explained.

Kerry and I glanced at each other. "The phone," I said.

"What phone?" Eddie demanded.

"Neil has access to Nathan's location through his phone. We found out yesterday it had some tracker on it, which is how he found them at Loch Einich. Nathan was told last night that he had to leave the phone behind."

"But he's a kid, and let me guess, he didn't want to give up his games first and his mates second?" Eddie asked.

"Exactly," I answered grimly. "We need to find it and get rid of the bloody thing before it takes away any advantage we currently have."

"I'll leave that one with you. Be in touch soon."

Eddie hung up and I glanced at Kerry. "If we stop, we lose precious time, and Nathan could shift if he becomes angry at us, insisting he throws the phone."

"Leave it with me to sort," Kerry responded.

Chapter 10

Kerry

I was fuming. I couldn't believe that Nathan would put us at such risk, putting himself at risk, all for a blasted phone. Without pausing, I unclipped my seat belt and scrambled into the rear of the car. Ben slowed down a little, probably not wishing to see me flying backwards through the windscreen if he had to slam on the brakes for anything.

Once in the back seat, I started rummaging through Nathan's rucksack. I was glad he'd wanted to keep it near him. Trying to get to the boot of the car would have been a challenge.

"Kerry, put a seatbelt on!" Ben demanded from the front seat.

I dragged a belt across me and locked it in place, without stopping the search. There was nothing in his rucksack, even though I double checked that I hadn't missed anything.

Looking at Nathan, there was no other choice but to try to search him. This time, I didn't go in as roughly as I had when searching his bag; if possible, I didn't want to wake him. He didn't murmur when I located the phone in the pocket nearest to the door, and I managed to retrieve it without waking him.

"Got it," I said, immediately pressing the button to release the window. Before it was open fully, I launched the phone as hard as I could out of the vehicle. We were travelling so fast that there was no time to see where it landed.

"What's happening?" Nathan shouted, having been woken suddenly by the noise of the air rushing in through the window. "Aunty Kerry, what have you done?"

Pressing the button to close the window and reduce the noise inside the car substantially, I turned to Nathan. "How could you, Nathan? How could you be so foolish as to keep your phone? We've been followed the whole time! The advantage we had at the start has been ruined because you were selfish, and I don't understand why you would be."

I was calm and consoling around him usually, fearful that if he was upset, he would shift and he would cause chaos, which would bring him to the attention of the authorities, but I couldn't help shouting at him. I was furious, and after the stress of the day, I had cursed him without holding back.

"But—"

"Nathan, don't you dare shift, and do not try to excuse yourself out of this situation, which has been one of your own making," Ben's voice reverberated around the car interior. It's strange to say, but it almost bounced off the seats.

Nathan had looked as if he was going to argue with me, but at Ben's words, he sank in his seat. "I won't."

"We are taking you to a community which is threatened by the wider world," Ben continued, his tone still authoritative and angry. "They are prepared to take you in as one of their own, when, apart from your aunt, the only person who wants you is someone who will make a lot of money by handing you over to a set of disreputable scientists. If they take you in, you'll spend the rest of your life being tested on while they try to work out what makes you different from the rest of us and how they can use it to their advantage. If you want that, be my guest; say the word now and I'll stop this car and hand you over without argument. If you are old enough to go against our advice, you're certainly old enough to make your own decisions. What's it to be, Nathan? Do I stop, or do I carry on?" Ben demanded.

He had never made eye contact with Nathan, but when Ben was speaking, Nathan had shrunk into himself, seeming smaller and younger. His eyes hadn't met mine; he'd just lowered his head and kept his eyes down.

"I'm sorry," he mumbled.

"What was that?" Ben demanded.

"I'm sorry. I've been stupid. I don't need my phone and I don't want Uncle Neil to catch up with us," he said, his head still lowered.

"Good. I don't want any more nonsense, or I will walk away from this whole situation, and you will be responsible for protecting your aunt. Is that clear?" Ben demanded.

"Yes, sir."

It was a good thing Nathan wasn't looking at me, for I genuinely believe my eyes were going to pop out of their sockets. *Sir*? He'd never used that term in his life before, I was sure of it. To say that today was a day of revelations was the understatement of the year.

I waited to see if anything else would be said, but it was clear that Nathan wasn't going to move from his curled-up position. Then it struck me – he was being submissive towards Ben. Of course! I don't know why I hadn't realised it the moment Nathan realised what Ben was. As far as a younger, weaker animal was concerned, Ben was alpha. It didn't matter that they were different species, and let's face it, there could be a tiger in Nathan's repertoire at some point in the future. I hadn't thought he could turn into a bird, but he had done.

I climbed back into the front seat and glanced over at Ben. He winked at me and I couldn't help smiling in return. He'd been playing a game in some respects, although I was sure that if Nathan had been belligerent, there would have been further repercussions, but I was grateful to him – he'd handled it perfectly.

When we eventually arrived at Gill's Bay, I realised how remote it was. There was a ferry terminal building, a large corrugated domed building and a small, ancient out-of-use brick building, and that was it. It was about as open and unprotected as it could get, and my stomach sank. Even if we'd managed to dodge Neil, the moment he came in sight of this tiny harbour, we would be seen.

The thoughts increased my nerves, and as if he could sense it, Ben squeezed my hand in reassurance. "Don't worry. I'm going to run into the ferry building and ask about parking my car out of sight."

"What are you going to say?"

"I'm a police officer, of another force, yes, but we do enquiries in other areas," Ben answered.

"You're on a career break!"

"They don't know that." He grinned as he got out of the car, stretched in a very cat-like way and then jogged over to the utilitarian building.

It was only a few moments before he came back, a smile on his face.

"I take it, they believed whatever you told them?" I asked with a raised eyebrow.

"Of course. We can store my car in the shed over there until I need to use it on my return, and we can wait in the staff room of the ferry building. It seems the Stroma residents have a network of people on the mainland, one of which happens to work here," Ben said.

"Don't you think that's a bit of a coincidence?" I asked.

"It's extra protection for them. They can assess, perfectly legitimately, who is trying to get off the mainland and in what, if they aren't using the official ferry."

"We aren't using the ferry."

"No, and our friend inside has said he's going to radio the boat waiting offshore to let them know that we've arrived early, and they'll send their smaller dinghy for us," Ben explained as he drove the car out of sight.

Letting a breath out slowly, I could only thank my lucky stars that I'd come across Ben, or that he'd come across us when he had. He made everything we had to do seem so easy, and I was unbelievably grateful to him.

"We'll soon be on the island," Ben said, before turning to look at Nathan, still seated in his submissive position. "Are you sure about this, Nathan? If you have second thoughts, we drive away from here now and I will give you my word that I will try my damnedest to keep you out of your uncle's grasp."

I looked in surprise at him. This was a change from what he'd said earlier. "But—" I started.

"It has to be Nathan's decision," Ben said. "He will be on an island for goodness knows how long, away from all he's known in the past. If he has any doubts, now is the time to raise them. There's still time to put things in place to dodge the dastardly Uncle Neil."

"No. I want to go," Nathan said, finally looking up. "I don't want to feel like an outsider all my life. I just wish Aunty Kerry could stay there with me."

I blinked away the tears his words caused. "Me too, little wolf," I said.

"She won't be thrown off as soon as you get there, and she's going to be allowed to visit you. As you grow, there will be places on the mainland you can meet. It will just be longer before you come over this side than it would normally be because of Neil."

"I know," Nathan said. "He's caused so much trouble. He's made everything so much harder, even when Mum was alive."

For the second time in as many minutes, I swallowed a lump in my throat. We'd tried to hide a lot of what Neil was doing from Nathan, as he was going through enough, but it seemed he'd still picked up quite a bit.

"Hopefully it will get better from now on," I said.

"You still want to stay with me for now, don't you?" Nathan asked.

"Of course, little wolf. You're my family and the most important person in my life." My words caused a swirling in my stomach, because there was someone else who was also very important to me, and he would leave us very soon; I was dreading it.

"Come on, let's get over to the ferry building," Ben said. "I would imagine it won't be long before our rescuers arrive."

Gathering our luggage, we crossed the empty car park. As we approached the ferry building, we heard the sound of an outboard motor, at which Ben veered to the side to see who was approaching. Turning to me with a nod, my stomach lurched with hope. This was it – safety.

Two men were manning the boat, one jumping out before the boat had reached the harbour side. He pulled the boat in and secured it to a harbour-side ring.

"Nathan?" he asked as he approached us.

"Yes," Nathan answered, but I could tell he was wary.

"I'm Malc and this is Steve. We're on the council." Malc turned to me. "Had a tough journey here?"

"Yes. My brother has followed us all the way and could be on our tail now," I admitted.

"Let's get going then," Malc said. "The main boat is further out. It's far more comfortable than the dinghy, but this lets us get in and out quickly. And who are you?" he asked, turning to Ben.

"Police officer, private investigator and in the right place at the right time," Ben answered, holding his hand out in greeting.

"And a large animal to boot," Malc said, shaking his hand. "There aren't many of you about."

"No. Or you, so I'm led to believe."

"True. Are you joining us?"

I glanced at Ben in alarm; I hadn't thought for a second that he would leave us here. Ben looked at me and smiled. "Is it ok if I join you? I'd like to see Nathan settled and I admit to being curious," he said.

"We aren't a freak show," Malc said tersely.

Ben held his hands up. "I'd never come across anyone with your talent until I met Nathan, but I might do in my private investigation work. It would be useful to know how to contact you in the future."

"Please come with us," I said quickly. "If that's ok?" I asked Malc.

"Yes. Let's get a move on then," Malc said, lifting our luggage into the boat and then handing us in.

Nathan sat close to me. I could sense his unease and wrapped my arm around him. Ben leaned over and patted Nathan on the knee. "Practise your breathing, Nathan. You've had a stressful day. I know this will be hard, but we're nearly there."

Nathan nodded and Ben moved away, but he'd squeezed my shoulder in reassurance.

Malc nodded to Nathan. "Not had the chance to shift today?" he asked.

"No, apart from very early in the morning, but he had to stay inside. My brother forced our hand and we had to get here as soon as we could," I admitted.

"As soon as we get on the island, you can shift and go and explore," Malc said to Nathan. "Burn some of that energy off while I show your aunt where you'll be staying and then the cottage she'll be in."

"Thank you." Nathan looked brighter at Malc's words, which I was grateful for. I really didn't want Nathan to feel uncomfortable, so that he wouldn't do something that might put him at a disadvantage.

Our attention was drawn to the boat anchored off the shoreline. It was far bigger than the dinghy we were on, but it wasn't ocean-going. It resembled a fishing trawler, but with fewer pieces of equipment on board. It certainly looked sturdy enough to handle the seas off northern Scotland.

After clambering on board, the dinghy was hoisted hydraulically to the back and then we were off once more. Every time I turned around and saw the land getting smaller, I breathed easier. Neil was not following us; it seemed we had done it.

We had been on the boat a while when we started to see the buildings on the island. I shot Ben a glance of alarm. "It's derelict," I whispered, suddenly wondering if we had walked from one nightmare into another.

We could see the shells of houses, all in various states of collapse. There was no sign of people or animals. My heart started to pound as the panic set in.

Malc lifted his hand as if in a wave, but there was no one there. Ben approached Malc. "What's going on? This isn't what we expected."

Malc grinned at him. "The island was abandoned years ago and fell into disrepair. This is what everyone sees as they sail past."

"But?" Ben persisted.

"We had the help of a few powerful witches when the island community was set up. You'll see what I mean when we get closer."

I hoped he was right, but remained close to Nathan. I had no idea what I could do, but I would try to protect him if needed. Ben moved over to stand near us; he took hold of my hand and squeezed it gently. It was a kind gesture and I was grateful for it. I knew without doubt he was aware of my fears, and his signal had been that I wasn't alone. It really helped.

The boat slowed down as we approached the island, and at the point when Malc turned to look at us with a grin on his face, it was as if we'd walked under an invisible curtain and come out in a different dimension – the island was so different. There were more buildings than we had seen, and well-kept gardens were everywhere, as were rows of houses. In the centre of the island were a few larger buildings. People were milling around, going about their everyday lives, completely unconcerned by our arrival as we approached the two figures who stood on the jetty.

"Relaxed now, have you?" Malc grinned at me. "Everyone feels the same as you did; there's nothing to worry about. You're safe here."

"What happens if another boat approaches the curtain?" I asked.

"You saw me wave? Well, it wasn't just a simple wave," Malc admitted. "It's the only signal which will get you through the barrier, and it's only those who work on the boat who know about it."

"What does anyone else see? Do they bounce off the magic?"

"No. It's set up so that if they reach the island, they can get off their boat and walk around, but they feel a deep unease and discomfort. It's usually only about half an hour before they're heading towards the mainland again, feeling far better once they've left than they did on the island."

"I bet there's all sorts of speculation about ghosts and ghouls," Ben said.

"You know what the non-magics are like – full of imagination when it suits them and completely unaccepting of anything different when it doesn't," Malc answered.

I could understand Malc's bitterness, although to be fair, it wasn't just non-magics who had been unaccepting in Nathan's case. We climbed off the boat and Malc gave Nathan a nod, which had him stripping down, no longer seeming shy about undressing in front of a group of strangers.

Shifting into a wolf, he gave an excited yap in my direction and then shot off across the grass. Two other wolves soon joined him, and after nose sniffs and a few growls, they all scampered off together.

Malc looked at me. "I primed two of our lads who are just a little older than Nathan at fourteen. They waited out of sight to see what animal he changed into so they could match him. We know he'll enjoy a run and tumble as part of a small gang."

"That's really considerate," I said.

Malc had seemed to be quite dour, but he smiled at me. "We've done this a time or two – we know what works by now. If you'd like to follow me, I can give you a more sedate exploration than Nathan is getting." Malc took us to the school building first. "We have structure each day, just as he would have in a mainstream school. He will have the same exams when he reaches sixteen and eighteen as he would if he was on the mainland."

"What about university?" I asked. It was a long way off, but I was already trying to work out finances in case Nathan needed it.

"Normally, they would be given a back story and then sent to the mainland to go to university just like any other student. With Nathan's situation, we might have to assess it when he decides what he wants to do. We wouldn't send him somewhere which would put him in danger from his uncle," Malc explained.

"Do you give instructions about their shifter status?" Ben asked.

"Yes. We have small class sizes, which enable us to achieve high results in less time. It means that part of the day is spent practising controlling their instincts and getting to the bottom of how many animals are within them and which one they would prefer to be," Malc explained.

"Does choosing cause conflict with the other animals?" Ben asked. "I know when I do something my tiger disagrees with, it makes its feelings known."

I wondered what he meant and if it was painful. It was fascinating to listen to them both speaking, far different from researching on the internet.

"To be fair, the dominant animal usually emerges naturally, but that doesn't mean to say that if the person doesn't want to be that animal, he or she can't suppress it; they just have to work a little harder. Many times it's the first animal which has appeared," Malc explained.

"It was a wolf with Nathan, although he has shifted into a bear a few times," I explained.

"He has lots of time before he needs to make a decision. While he is on this island, he can let his animals roam free. We learn control techniques to help when needed."

"He's going to be a powerful beast," Ben said. "We'd been out for a long run yesterday, and when at risk, he managed to shift into a buzzard for the first time and get himself to safety."

"Really? That's interesting. There aren't many of us who can shift into birds; he is clearly going to be a special case. It will be an honour nurturing him."

"He won't be victimised because of it, will he?" I'm the anxious aunt. I could see they both thought that, but I couldn't help my concern.

"He'll more likely be spoiled because of it," Malc said with a slight smile. "Being different is something to be proud of on this island. Come, I'll show you where Nathan will be staying."

"He won't be staying with me?"

"No. We have all the children staying together, like a boarding school during the week, but they return home on weekends. Nathan has been allocated to my house. My wife and two little girls are looking forward to having a big brother around the place," Malc explained.

"Oh, I didn't think I'd have to say goodbye so soon." Ben slipped his hand into mine and I squeezed the large hand, gripping onto it like a lifeline.

"There's no hurry for you to leave, but it will be better for Nathan if you don't stay around too long. You are more than welcome to visit for the whole of the school holidays if you wish, but remember he will be setting up a life here; he'll be with those who are the same as him. He needs a sense of belonging, and initially seeing you will probably make him more unsettled. I'm sorry. I know it's hard when he hasn't come from a shifting family. A shifter needs to feel like they belong – it is an overwhelming drive."

"But you're a lone animal," I said to Ben, grasping at straws that Nathan would want to be with me more than these people who were offering him sanctuary. It was selfish of me, I know, but it felt like I was losing Nathan and Viv at the same time.

"I am, but even I am joining with my friends who are the same animal as I am. We gravitated towards each other at university," Ben said, looking at me with sympathy, but continuing the gentle pressure of support on my hand.

"He could decide he wishes to return to you when everything has been sorted out with his uncle, but these first couple of years will be him finding out who he is and where he fits in the shifter world," Malc said.

"I appreciate your reassurance and I do understand. I might not like it, but I can fully comprehend the need to belong," I said.

"Good. I'll show you your house," Malc said, taking us down a few streets after he'd shown us the boarding school block. "The island is large enough that we can stretch our legs whichever beast we are," he explained as he walked. "But we do take groups off to some of the other, remote islands when we want a change of scenery. We also go back to the mainland quite a bit, although Nathan won't be able to until it is safe for him. We aren't normally restricted by living here."

"It is a beautiful place," I said, and I meant it. The sea could be seen from almost every spot, and it had the beauty that can only be found in a rugged landscape. I had seen what seemed to be sand in a couple of the coves when we were approaching the island, but the wind blustering across the landscape was relentless.

"It is, but it can get really chilly in the winter. We spend a lot of time shifted when it's too cold, or the snow comes. It's more fun with a fur coat wrapped around you," Malc said. "Here we are – it's only small, but it should have everything you need."

We were standing outside a pretty grey stone house; it had a door and a window on the ground floor, and two windows on the first floor. There was smoke coming out of the chimney and it had a welcome feel about it.

"You never said how much I owe you for staying," I said.

"Nothing. We are self-sufficient as an island, taking some of our wares to the mainland to sell," Malc explained. "Others are lucky enough that we can work from home. We all contribute to the upkeep of the island, and we have residents who have moved away but still support their home."

"It sounds perfect."

"Oh, don't worry. We bicker like every other group of people, but ultimately, we know what we have here is special, and no one puts that at risk."

A woman came out of the house, walked over with a smile on her face and hugged me. I was a bit surprised at the overly familiar greeting, but I couldn't help smiling at her words. "Welcome to the island. I'm Bev, Malc's wife. We can't wait to welcome Nathan into our home; he's going to be spoiled as if he were our own son."

"Thank you, that means a lot." It did, but I also felt the feeling of real loss at losing the only family member I had left who I loved dearly.

"Come in and let's get you warmed up. I saw the three boys chasing by here about ten minutes ago – they seemed to be having a right old time of it. Nathan will be shattered when he gets back. I've made cake for his return," Bev said.

"That is definitely the way to get to Nathan's heart," I said with a smile, warming immediately to the woman, who I knew instinctively would look after Nathan well.

"It still works with Malc," Bev said with a grin as she led the way into the cosy house.

"Oi! Don't tell all my secrets," Malc said from the rear.

"I'm only telling her what she'll already know from being with her own shifter. Keep feeding him sweet things and it keeps him full of energy for every aspect of life."

She let out a crack of laughter at my flushed cheeks, and I dared not glance at Ben, as she'd obviously misinterpreted what we were, although I did notice that neither of us was keen to correct her mistake.

Chapter 11

Ben

Malc and Bev had stayed with us long after Nathan had returned. He'd fallen asleep as soon as he'd sat on the sofa, and they'd remained with us until he'd woken up a couple of hours later. They'd told us all about the history of the island and the community, and some of the good and bad stories of being a multiple shifter, or multi-shifter, as they called themselves.

Nathan had woken, still sleepy but hungry, and had shyly greeted Bev, obviously having found out a little of what was going on. He'd eaten almost half of the cake which had been made for his arrival, and only stopped when Bev had asked if he wanted to go and see his new room in their home and meet his new sisters. He'd looked at Kerry and I could see he was torn – excited about his new adventure, but not wanting to upset her.

She was clearly upset, but tried to hide it from him, not wishing to spoil his excitement at being with his own kind. Hugging him, she told him to go off and she'd see him in the morning. Nathan had left with Malc, while Bev hung back a little.

"He'll be fine. Don't feel he's leaving you behind; you are welcome to stay as long as you want," she said to Kerry, hugging her.

"I know, and thank you," Kerry said, but her voice was strangled.

"We'll see you tomorrow. Our house is number twelve Beachfront Crescent. Come down for lunch and you can see the set-up we have."

Kerry smiled and I walked Bev to the door in the small house. "Try to convince her not to worry," Bev said to me in a whisper. "It's going to be harder for Kerry in many ways."

"I know," I responded.

"Look after her; she's clearly a gem," Bev said, and with a pat on my arm, she was on her way.

Closing the door, I returned to find Kerry staring blindly into the fire. I could see she was struggling not to cry. Walking across to her, I sat next to her on the small two-seater sofa and put my arm around her shoulders. I didn't say anything – what could I say? This was the start of her having to leave Nathan behind.

She stiffened initially at my touch and I was going to pull away. I wasn't going to force comfort on her if she didn't want it, but she surprised me by grabbing hold of my shirt, leaning into my chest and bursting into tears.

I felt a little helpless. I've never been good with crying – what are you supposed to do? Speak? Offer inane platitudes or join in? I've never quite worked it out.

In the end, I just rubbed her back and waited until she stopped of her own accord. She eventually moved away slightly, burying her head in her hands and groaning.

"Your shirt," she moaned through her fingers.

"It is a bit soggy, but it's fine. I'm used to far worse when I'm running through the snow, don't forget, and I shift into my naked form – a few tears on my shirt is fine," I assured her.

"That's not a few tears, it's a tsunami. I'm sorry."

"Don't be. Shall we get some food, and then we can open the bottle of wine Bev left for us? I think you deserve a relaxing night after the day you've had." I busied myself getting out pasta and chopping ham, peppers and mushrooms, which had been kindly left in the well-stocked fridge.

"Thank you for today. Again. We would have never made it without your help, and Eddie, of course," Kerry said, joining me in the kitchen area and uncorking the bottle of wine and pouring two glasses.

"Happy to help, and I've been able to see this island as a community I didn't know existed. I feel quite ignorant, but they certainly seem to have everything worked out." The thing which struck me about the island was that it almost felt like one big home. The others on the boat and in the ferry terminal had been welcoming and helpful. It was in stark contrast to what I'd experienced as a shifter and had ignited the ache which I normally managed to suppress.

I was a lone animal, but that didn't mean a part of me didn't long to belong to something – a family. That's what I'd always longed for, and now my tiger was getting increasingly frustrated with the lack of a mate to create a family of our own. Unfortunately for me, it wasn't as simple as my animal seemed to think. How could I hope to offer the love and support children needed when I had never experienced it myself?

Rousing myself, I accepted the glass of wine from Kerry and took a sip. "Why don't we get up early and go for a walk around the island?" I suggested. "Get a real look at it before everyone is awake."

"That sounds like a good idea. I saw beaches which looked nice, although they'll be chilly," Kerry answered. "Will you not need to go for a run on your own first? So your animal can stretch its legs?"

It pleased me that she'd considered my needs, and I smiled at her. "If you don't mind carrying a rucksack with my clothes in, we could do both at the same time?" I watched her carefully. She'd seen me shift and had spent most of a night sleeping beside my tiger, but that had been when she had been worried. Although she was still concerned about leaving Nathan, she was no longer frightened for their safety and she might not wish to get up close and personal with my beast.

She flushed a little and I thought she was going to say no, but she surprised me by responding, "Yes, ok."

"Good. I hope you like getting up early."

"Does anyone?" Kerry responded.

"Yes, it's the best time of day."

"You're odd."

"It's been said before," I admitted. That had been different, though; the words hadn't been said teasingly, nor with a smile which made her eyes sparkle. I had the urge always to make her smile, but pushed it away. She had enough going on without me making a move on her.

When the food was ready, we both moved to the sofa and sat next to each other, tucking into the steaming pasta dish.

Kerry eventually put her bowl down and rubbed her stomach. "I'm full," she groaned.

"I forget that not everyone has the metabolism of a shifter," I admitted.

"Good skin and a fast metabolic rate – it gets more unfair as I find out more," she said with arched eyebrows.

"I'd say sorry, but I'm not," I grinned in response.

"And I thought you were a true gentleman," Kerry said.

I snorted. "My father, should you ever have the misfortune to meet him, would have you believe I'm the lowest of the low, nothing to recommend me to any decent person."

"He sounds delightful," Kerry said. "What is it about families?"

"The problem starts when you can't pick them," I pointed out. "I certainly wouldn't have chosen my father, that's for sure. Mum is a typical mum, though."

There was no point in trying to explain how even that relationship had collapsed when it mattered.

"My parents were great. I can't imagine how Neil turned out the way he did, and Viv to a lesser extent, although I always feel disloyal saying that about her because I loved her dearly and we were very close."

"Acknowledging someone's faults doesn't mean you feel any less for them."

"No. I suppose not, although that wasn't the case with Dan," Kerry said with a grimace.

"Another relative?" I asked the question even though I knew instinctively he wasn't.

"No. Nearly, I suppose. A fiancé, and a rubbish one when it came down to it. I suppose it was better to know before we got married, but it hurt at the time. I have to think that it's all in the past now."

My tiger was growling at the thought of her with someone else. I surreptitiously rubbed my chest, trying to calm the beast. I felt the same stab of jealousy as he was, which was ridiculous when you considered I'd only known her for a few days, but it was intense nonetheless.

"What happened?" I wasn't sure I wanted to hear the whole story, yet I was compelled to ask. Why not increase the suffering? Sometimes I'm a complete fool, but the words were out and I couldn't take them back.

"The cracks started to show when I started spending more time with Viv and Nathan when we first realised he wasn't the usual kind of shifter we'd heard about. He had little understanding that I would want to support my sister and nephew. Apparently, calling in two to three times a week on my way home from work and ringing every day was bordering on an unhealthy obsession by me," she admitted. "It could have been seen as such, I suppose, in fairness to him."

"You were experiencing something unheard of in the wider population, and she was a single mother – of course, you would help," I defended her. "I would have probably been there every night."

Kerry smiled. "I probably would have been if I hadn't had to deal with Dan moaning so much every day. If we'd been living separately, it wouldn't have been so obvious, but we'd moved in to save up for a deposit on a house."

"What happened when your sister died?"

"That's when it really blew up," she said bitterly. "I'd spent the first few days with Nathan at Viv's house. I didn't want to take him away from his home immediately, but I intended to move him in with us when he was ready to. Then I received an ultimatum from Dan, via text, saying that if I didn't return home by the end of the week – alone – the wedding was off. Needless to say, the wedding was called off within an hour of receiving the text."

"Good for you." I increased the pressure of my hand on my chest.

Kerry looked questioningly at me. "Are you ok?"

I groaned. This could be awkward. Thinking on my feet, I smiled slightly. "It's my tiger; he's really annoyed that your boyfriend didn't support you when you needed it most. Let's just say it feels like he's pacing around inside me and his snarling makes my chest rumble." It was the best I could think of without telling her the truth – that my tiger and I wanted to rip his head off, not only for being unsupportive but for not being nearly good enough for her.

"It must feel very strange."

"It's something you get used to, eventually."

"Nice of your tiger, though," Kerry said.

Great, now the bloody tiger was winning points, something which caused him to rumble in pleasure.

"May I?" Kerry asked, stretching her hand out towards my chest. Her cheeks flushed a little and I nodded, wondering what she was going to do, but I certainly wasn't going to miss the chance of being touched by her. "Hey, Mr Tiger, thanks for the concern," she said, rubbing my chest gently. "I'm well rid of him, but it's nice to know you would have been on my side."

"We both would have been," I responded when she moved her hand in a stroking motion, smiling bashfully. Ok, I was acting like a little child, jumping up and saying, 'Me too! Me too!' "You've got him purring now."

Kerry laughed, clearly embarrassed, but she also looked pleased. I acknowledged that my tiger had won that round. As he wanted her as his mate, I wasn't really annoyed with him – the more I got to know her, the more I wanted the same. A pity I wouldn't be acting on my feelings; she had enough going on.

"He's looking forward to exploring the island with you," I admitted.

"I hope he doesn't expect me to keep up with him! Especially after a few glasses of wine and the early start we had this morning. It feels like it's been the longest of days," she admitted, stifling a yawn. "Sorry."

"Come on. I'm being selfish; you're exhausted. Let's get an early night and you'll feel better in the morning." The fact that the words 'early night' made my mind wander to more pleasurable pursuits than sleeping caused my insides to stir, but I pushed the thoughts aside. This was not the time for romance; it was the time for looking after someone who was vulnerable and needed support.

"I'm not such a lightweight normally. I promise to take you for a drink after all this is done and show you that I can hold my own," Kerry said.

Her words gave me a little hope that she might be interested in me if she was considering meeting up when she'd left the island. "One tip," I said, standing and moving over to take our glasses to wash them out. "Don't ever get in a drinking competition with a shifter."

"Let me get this right – you have perfect skin, heal quickly, don't put on weight and can hold your drink?" she asked, following me to the kitchen area.

"That about sums it up," I admitted.

"Tell me you've had a hangover. Please."

"I've had a hangover."

"You're lying, aren't you?"

"Yes."

"For goodness sake! I'm with your friend Jenny – it's just not fair!" she huffed.

"I can fall asleep instantly, too."

"I think you'd better stop now. I am rapidly changing my opinion of you."

"Oh, really? I can't let that happen. I'm shutting up."

"Just be grateful you have within you a cute tiger," she said, walking towards the door.

My laughter followed her as she disappeared into the inner hallway. My tiger was disgusted at her words. "She obviously considers you a helpless kitten," I said, antagonising my beast. Don't worry, he got his own back, going on an inner rampage for the next hour, until I apologised. Some beasts just can't take a joke.

Chapter 12

Kerry

I woke up when Ben knocked on the door. "Coffee in ten minutes," he said through the closed door.

Rolling over with a groan, I buried my head in my pillow before realising it wasn't fair to make him wait. Muttering to myself that people who needed to get up before dawn should be avoided at all costs, I had a quick shower and dressed in warm clothing. The island looked beautiful, but it was located in the North Sea, so it was probably bitterly cold.

Ben greeted me with a smile; he looked refreshed and wide awake. I couldn't help the glower I aimed in his direction, at which he laughed and handed me a coffee and a plate of toast. "I'll cook us something nice when we return," he said. "This is just to keep you going."

As I munched the toast, I wondered if he was the most perfect man who had ever been created. I'd been attracted to him physically from the moment I saw him. I challenge even the most devoted nuns not to appreciate the looks and physique he had.

The problem – even though it was a ridiculous problem to have – was that he's a lovely man. He'd gone above and beyond what even a close friend would do, let alone the stranger he was, over these last couple of days, and I couldn't stop thinking about him. I was doing my best not to behave like some soppy teenager around him constantly.

Yes, I was concerned about Nathan, Neil, and what I was going to do in the future, but I was also trying to work out how I could make sure that I kept in touch with this amazing man once I'd left the island. My feeble attempt last night at inviting him on a night out hadn't exactly been grasped by him wanting to set a date for it, but then again, he didn't know when I'd be leaving the island, or where I was going to be. For that matter, I had no idea where he would be living, and for the first time in all this mess, I didn't necessarily want to stay in this remote part of Scotland if it meant I would never see Ben again. I silently cursed myself for being selfish, but those were my feelings. Perhaps I wasn't too dissimilar to my selfish brother and sister after all. That was a depressing thought to start the day with!

"You can change your mind if you don't want to come," Ben said, dragging me out of my thoughts.

"What makes you say that?"

"You looked unhappy. I don't want to force you to do something you don't want to."

"I was thinking about my family. Sorry, I'm not really a morning person, especially when there is a fine line between this being morning and the middle of the night," I answered.

"It's the best time of the day," Ben responded with a grin, picking up his rucksack. "Time to go."

I followed him, and we walked to the first beach, where he was in human form. He chatted along the way, the torchlight illuminating the path ahead of us. I certainly knew what the term dark sky meant when walking along; the sun hadn't started to rise and the sky was pitch dark.

When we walked onto the beach, we were sheltered a little and I was able to stand and watch the foam on top of the waves as they broke onto the sand. It looked strange, staring into the darkness of the sea, unable to see anything beyond a few feet.

"It's so peaceful here. I am a little concerned that Nathan will find it boring – teenagers like entertainment and noise," I admitted.

"I think he'll be kept too busy to be bored. He's got lots of lives to live as he shifts into his different animals," Ben said. "Do you mind if I shift now? I will be running around to start with, but I won't be too far away."

"Of course, and don't worry about me – I feel perfectly safe here," I admitted.

He stood behind me while he undressed and shifted, even though I'd seen him without clothes on before. I didn't know whether to be pleased that he was always the gentleman or disappointed that I didn't get a peek at his fine body.

124

Once his tiger sprang away and across the beach, I packed everything into the rucksack and put it on my shoulders. Walking across the sand in the direction Ben had run, I took my time, enjoying being alone. It seemed an age since I hadn't been in Nathan's company for fear of what Neil might do, and I could just think of nothing except how beautiful the island was.

For such a small island, the beach curved around the land in a wide arc. I followed, using the torch until the slowly rising sun started to lighten the night sky. Ben kept running in large circles around the area, regularly coming back to me, but not getting too close. He even splashed through the seawater, which was brave as it must have been freezing.

We had walked about three miles, in Ben's case far more, when he turned back the way we'd come. An hour had passed and the sky was a lot brighter. Morning hadn't fully arrived, but there was no need to use the torch as I had been doing, so it had been packed with Ben's clothes in the rucksack. I occasionally saw other animals in the distance, but no one approached us. I think they were all enjoying their solitude and the vast expanse of land, just as we were.

Ben joined me in tiger form and walked alongside me for a few moments. I put my hand on his shoulder as he walked. It felt as glorious as it had when I first touched him when he was guarding us. Thick and warm, I could feel his body move with the deep breaths he was taking; he was almost pulsing with energy.

Glancing at me, he stopped walking and crouched down, looking at me sideways.

"Do you want to sit here?" I asked. Nudging my hand, I could have sworn he shook his head. "No? If you think I'm racing you, I'm not that stupid," I said, trying to interpret what the sort of crouch meant.

My comment received a snort of disgust, and he moved around me, nudging my knees from behind. I started to walk, at which I heard a growl as he quickly moved in front of me and then stopped.

"What?" I asked in frustration, at which he backed into me a little way. Suddenly having a suspicion I'd guessed what he wanted me to do, I backed away. "Oh no! If you think you can carry my weight on you, you have completely misjudged how heavy I am. I'd break your back."

Receiving a huff, he walked around me again, this time trying to get me to sit on him from behind. He was being persistent, and I must admit that although I was concerned about the practicalities of carrying me, the thought of doing as he suggested was piquing my curiosity now he'd suggested it.

After another nudge, I turned to him. "Ok, on your head be it. If you have a bad back after this, don't moan to me!" He yawned loudly, which received a glare from me. "That's just rude when I'm trying to be considerate of you."

I could see the twinkle of amusement in his eyes. It was strange – it wasn't Ben, yet it so very much was.

Moving so I could climb on him as I would a horse, I wrapped my hands around his neck, trying to spread my weight. It felt scarily intimate to be so close to his face as I leaned across. I received a sideways look, which I took to be an enquiry as to whether I was ready.

"Do your worst, tiger," I said with a laugh as he set off at a run.

I wasn't a horsewoman by any stretch of the imagination, although I had ridden horses, but this was nothing like it in comparison. Ben's movements were more fluid, graceful even, as he forged ahead across the sand. He never seemed to be affected by the movement underfoot as he ran, his large, padded paws acting as a perfect stabiliser. Being so close to his head, I could hear his heavy breathing and see the explosions of his hot breath on the cold morning air.

I started to stiffen when he turned towards the sea. "Oh, no, no!" I shouted into his ear, and I'm sure he let out a laugh before running into the smaller waves.

Squealing as the ice-cold splashes of water hit me as he ran through the edges of the waves, I sat up to escape some of the water. Grasping onto his fur, Ben turned away from the sea and struck out once more across the beach.

It was utterly exhilarating. I couldn't stop the laugh escaping as we rushed across the beach. In a moment of utter abandon, I let go of Ben's fur and opened my arms, letting the cold air slap across my body as we travelled.

Ben picked up the speed until I clung to him once more, when he slowed and came almost to a stop. At the last minute, he tilted his body, and I fell on the sand.

"You beast," I laughed. "I'm covered in seawater and you've just made sure I'll be covered in sand too."

Turning to face me, he licked my cheek with his rough tongue, which made me laugh louder. Wrapping my arms around his head, I kissed his nose. "Thank you," I said and then flopped on the sand.

Ben shifted as I lay and flopped, still undressed, next to me. He was breathing heavily, but a huge grin was on his face. "That seems to have woken you up."

"It was brilliant. I wish I had the freedom to run as fast and as unrestrained as that every day," I admitted.

"Whenever you want a repeat performance, just ask," Ben said. He was lying close and although we weren't touching, it felt very intimate.

"Your back might regret you uttering those words. You haven't tried walking yet," I countered. I was trying to keep things light. I wanted to reach out and touch him, but felt nervous about doing anything he might reject.

"You're nothing but a slip of a thing," Ben said.

"You shouldn't tell such outrageous lies," I said, punching his arm. I didn't seem to be able to stop myself from touching him in some form.

"I don't tell lies," he said, leaning up on his elbow and looking down at me.

Swallowing, I smiled at him. This was it, he was going to kiss me and I couldn't wait for it to happen. He leaned forward a little, and then his phone rang in the side pocket of the rucksack.

"Damn, I'm going to have to answer that," he said, moving away and grabbing the bag.

He hadn't been touching me, but I felt colder when he moved away. Sitting up, I saw his expression change when he saw who was ringing on his phone's display. Moving away from me, he answered the call.

I could tell something was wrong; his whole stance was rigid. I couldn't hear what was being said – having turned away from me, the wind took his words – but I could tell it wasn't good.

Unpacking his rucksack of clothes, I tried not to panic. If it was about Nathan, I would have received the call, not him. I kept trying to convince myself. When the call ended, I stood waiting for him to turn back to me and tell me what was going on, but instead he shifted once more, let out an almighty roar and ran off away from me.

"Ben!" I shouted once, but I should have saved my breath, for I knew he wasn't going to turn back. Something had upset him and he wanted to be alone. I could understand that, but I was sorry I couldn't help.

Collecting his clothes once more, and his phone, which had fallen onto the sand once he'd shifted, I headed back to the cottage. The walk was over; it was time to face whatever the day was going to throw at us.

Nathan was waiting for me outside the cottage when I reached the door. "Hey, why didn't you ring me to say you were here? I could have got back earlier," I said as I opened the door and walked into the warm house. I was grateful for the heat; I still felt chilled from Ben being upset and not being able to help him.

"It's ok, I've only just got here. I've been exploring the island with my two new friends. We shifted as bears today," he said happily.

"I thought I saw bears at one point," I admitted. There had been wolves too, but no other tigers.

The change in him in only a few hours was marked and I smiled at him, ruffling his hair as he walked past me into the kitchen area. "Abandoning your wolf, are you?" I teased.

"No, but Will and Andy said that eventually I will settle on a favourite animal and shift into that most of the time," he answered.

"You'll always be my little wolf, even if you turn into an elephant."

He grinned. "I don't suppose you've got any food? I've had an early breakfast at Bev and Malc's, but I wouldn't say no to something else."

I opened the fridge and took out bacon and sausage. Bev had thought of everything. This really was a kindness with the amount of food they'd supplied, never mind everything else they'd done for us. "These do?"

"Oh yes."

Busying myself with the grill, I instructed him to get some toast on the go. "What are your plans today? Are you going to show me the island?" I asked.

"Could we do it later?" Nathan responded. "I don't need to start school yet, Malc said, but I'd like to go in for half a day. It's the best way to get to know the other kids on the island. I know I've met four – the two daughters of Bev and Malc are really cute. They stayed up late last night, asking me a lot of questions. Then we played board games, but they are younger than I am, at eight and ten. Malc says there are ten teenagers on the island and ten younger children. It'll be strange going to a school with only twenty kids in it."

I'd never seen Nathan like this. He was positively glowing; there was no repining for a screen to hide behind, playing inane games. I had felt a slight pang that I wouldn't be seeing much of him, but it was wonderful to see his excitement and calmness, as if he were at peace with the world.

"You do exactly what you want to. This is your adventure and new life," I said, flipping the bacon over.

"Thanks, Aunty Kerry. Bev said I had to include you in as much of island life as I could, but I knew you'd understand and not be clingy."

Laughing, I tutted. "I've got some bad news for you, little wolf. I'm going to cling to you until my dying day, so you'd better get used to it."

Rolling his eyes, he buttered the toast. "I know that. You're my most important family and always will be, but I like these other shifters – they seem really nice."

"Good to know," I said. It was a good thing I was facing away from him because I had to surreptitiously wipe away the tears his words caused, and I didn't want to make him uncomfortable in any way. This was exactly what I'd hoped would happen, and I know Viv would have been over the moon to know he was safe and settled.

We sat down to eat, and when we'd finished, Nathan washed up. I took the opportunity to broach a subject which, after the conversation we'd just had, I thought it was an appropriate time to mention.

"When are you thinking you'd like me to leave the island?" I asked.

Nathan swung around from the sink. "You aren't thinking of going just yet, are you?" he demanded.

"No. But I also don't want to split you in two, trying to spend time with me while you're also settling in," I said gently.

"Could you just hang around for a few days?" he asked. "I'm not ready to say goodbye just yet."

"We will be in touch regularly. Don't think for one second you will be able to escape me even when I leave."

"Good. I know I'll have to stay on the island for quite a long time, but I hope you can come every school holiday at least."

"I'd better get a job which is term-time then," I grinned.

Nathan dried his hands, walked over to me and hugged me. "Thanks, Aunty Kerry. You've made everything ok for me."

"Anything for you, little wolf," I whispered.

The door opened and we parted as Ben walked into the house, naked.

"I have to leave the island today," he said, grabbing the rucksack and starting to get dressed.

Chapter 13

Ben

"Your mother is dead."

Four words that shook me to my core and tilted my world so unexpectedly that I struggled to breathe for a few moments.

"Are you there?" my father demanded.

"Yes."

"I want her stuff out of the house by the weekend, or it's going to the dump."

"It's Thursday!"

"I don't care. I want it out. If you want any of it, come and get it."

"Don't you think you should be telling me how she died and when?" I asked, not trying to hide the bitterness in my tone.

"Yesterday. Heart attack. No prior warning," came the terse reply. "If you come, you can stay in your grandmother's old house; you're not staying under this roof."

"I would never expect to. I'm fully aware of your opinion of me."

"Good. Then there's no misunderstanding. Are you coming, or should I throw the lot away?"

"You don't want anything of hers?"

"Of course I don't. I might have had to stay mated with her, but thankfully, that's ended. Now I can start my life. Are you coming or not?"

"Yes, I am, you heartless bas..." The phone line had gone dead before I'd finished the sentence.

I had never experienced fury mixed with despair; it felt like a physical pain. I couldn't turn around to Kerry. I couldn't let her see me upset – she needed me to be strong. I wouldn't be able to explain everything to her in any coherent way, so it was better to get away somewhere.

Shifting, I started to run; all thoughts of enjoying my time with Kerry disappeared. If that phone call had come thirty seconds later, I would have kissed her, but the moment had gone and probably forever, especially with the fact that I had to leave the island today.

Mum had died. As I pounded across the sand and then onto the grassland beyond the beach, the words echoed through my head. Dead. No going back, no repairing the damage which had been done.

I don't know how many miles I covered, but I eventually came to a stop at a cliff edge and flopped down, shifting as I sat. The cold didn't bother me; the heat I'd generated through the hard exercise coursing through my body would keep me warm.

The edge was about thirty feet above sea level, but I sat on it, my legs dangling over. I don't know whether it was a challenge to the gods to take me as well, or whether it was an act of desperation, but I think if the cliff had started to crumble at that moment, I wouldn't have fought to save myself.

My relationship with my father was non-existent, but with Mum, it was more complicated. We had been so very close; my chest ached when I thought back over my early years. They had been happy and uncomplicated. There was always tension between my father and me, which I hadn't understood, but Mum had always made up for it. When he wasn't around, which was often, we had the best of times.

The real trouble had begun when I'd started to shift. Nathan didn't realise how lucky he was to have someone fighting his corner as fiercely as his mum and then Kerry had done. It had taken my first shift to realise how delicate the relationships in my household were.

It's usual to have a small audience when you first shift, usually your parents, who can guide you and protect you as you make your first few transitions. They are uncomfortable to start with and so exhausting, just as Nathan had found out.

They'd known it was due, and thankfully, or so I thought, it happened at a weekend. Mum and Dad had been in the room, Mum encouraging me, Dad just watching, and the shift had happened. I'd felt amazing once I'd shifted, but could see immediately that something was amiss.

Dad stormed out of the house and Mum sat down and started to cry. I couldn't understand what was going on, not being fully in communication with my animal. I walked into the hallway, puzzled and unsure of what to do, and then walked past the hall mirror and realised what the problem was.

I was a tiger.

Managing to shift back to human form, I collapsed, exhausted, on the hall floor. I must have slept for hours, because it was dark when I woke up. I could still hear Mum crying, and I walked into the kitchen, questions buzzing. Dad had returned, probably stepping over my prone body to get into the house.

"What's happening?" I asked, in complete and utter confusion.

"You're moving into your grandma's house," Dad snapped, not looking at me.

"Mum?" I asked.

"It's better this way, at least for a while," Mum said, still sobbing.

"He won't be coming back. Can you imagine the scandal that this is going to cause once it gets out?" Dad hissed at her.

"Why am I a tiger and not a wolf?" I asked. Everyone knew if your parents were one animal, it passed down to the children. If there was a marriage between a shifter and a human, it wasn't always guaranteed that the child would be a shifter, so I might not have turned into a shifter, as my mother was human. It still meant that I should have followed my father's animal, which was a wolf. There could only be deviation if there was that particular animal within a family's history. Mine consisted of wolves and nothing else.

"Good question," Dad sneered, turning to Mum. "Why is he a tiger?"

Mum just cried louder and sobbed out, "I don't know."

"You're a damn lying bitch!" Dad said. I thought he was going to hit her, and I moved towards her to protect her. Dad laughed at the gesture. "Think you're Mr tough guy now, you're a bigger animal than me? I can still rip your throat out if you want to challenge me."

"No!" Mum cried out. "Ben, go and get your things and go to Grandma's. I'll see you later."

I did as I was bid, but life was never the same again, and Mum and I didn't return to our easy relationship. It had hurt and I'd felt betrayed when she'd supported Dad in everything he demanded after that day. I had left the area as soon as I could.

Looking out over the sea, I reflected on the years that had passed since then. I couldn't repine at the missed opportunities when nothing would have changed. The decision had been hers, and nothing anyone could have done or said would have changed her mind.

They were mates, my tiger whispered to me.

"Yes, and look what trouble it can cause," I answered, standing up. "I will never understand turning your back on your child when he was as confused and upset as I was. Surely part of being a mate is to protect the future offspring? It certainly didn't happen in our household."

He growled at the inference that I intended to back away from Kerry, but I couldn't think about any potential future with her. How could I risk my heart and soul to be put through the type of family life I'd already experienced? It was better to remain alone. Shifting once more, I headed back towards the house. It was time to return to the place which had not been home for almost two decades.

*

Hating that I'd interrupted a special moment between Kerry and Nathan, I just blurted out the words.

"Aww, no, Ben. I haven't shown you anything I've learned yet," Nathan said, but I noticed Kerry's look of shock, which was like yet another kick in the gut. It seemed today was the day for them.

"I'm sorry, pal. There's been a family death; I need to go. Could you go and ask Malc if I could have the boat take me over to the mainland?" I asked.

"'Course. Sorry, Ben," Nathan said. He didn't ask who'd died and I was glad. I didn't want him to be reminded of his own mother's death when he was so buoyant.

Kerry waited until Nathan had left the house and then approached me. "The phone call? Are you ok?"

"It's my mum," I said and struggled to hold back the tears which had flooded my eyes.

"Oh, Ben, I'm so sorry," Kerry said, immediately wrapping me in a hug.

Pulling her to me, I hadn't realised how much I'd needed physical contact until I was held tightly by her. "We weren't close," I muttered into her hair.

She pulled away a little, keeping her arms around me, but enough that she could look me in the eyes. "She was your mum; it doesn't matter how close you were to her or not. It must be devastating."

"I can't believe I'll never see her again," I choked, finally letting some of my distress into the open.

"Oh, Ben," she murmured, embracing me once more.

We only separated when Nathan and Malc came into the house. "Nathan's explained why you want to leave. There's a boat leaving in an hour. Will that do, or do you need it sooner?"

"An hour is fine, thank you," I responded. "It'll give me time to have a quick shower and go through a few things with Kerry before I go. Thanks for everything you're doing. It's an amazing set-up – I only wish there'd been enough time for me to explore further."

"You are welcome back at any point. You did well getting Nathan here, so there'll always be a place for you on the island."

We shook hands and I wondered if Malc had an inkling that I was a bit of a nomad. He encouraged Nathan to say his goodbyes and persuaded him to

140

return home with him. I was thankful for his tact. I wanted to talk to Kerry, and some of it would make Nathan worry when it was time for her to leave the island.

"I'll just gather my stuff together," I said, heading towards the bedrooms.

"I'll put some bacon and sausage on," Kerry said.

"Thanks. I'm going to book a flight from Inverness," I said.

"Where do you live?"

"My parents live in a village just outside Manchester, so it will be quicker for me to get home. I have to empty the house by Saturday of Mum's stuff."

Kerry frowned at my words. I couldn't blame her; they were strange, but I didn't have time to explain. Grabbing a quick shower and packing didn't take too long, and there was a welcome plate of food and a steaming cup of tea waiting for me when I returned to the kitchen.

"Thank you for this," I said, sitting on one of the barstools.

"Tell me to mind my own business if you like. I can understand you needing to return home, but why do you need to empty your mum's place so quickly? It seems a little soon," Kerry said.

I snorted. "You think? Yet, my so-called father is probably currently celebrating the fact that he's free from the binding marriage to my mother, if his words are anything to be believed."

"No! Surely not? If they weren't happy, why didn't they divorce?"

"Shifters mate for life," I said between mouthfuls. "Divorce isn't something we do, except in extreme circumstances. If a shifter hurts his or her mate, then a separation is allowed, but that's the only reason there would be a divorce."

"Oh."

"Yes, exactly. It means we are usually extremely careful in choosing a mate, but mistakes do happen."

"It'll be hard to face without support. Is there no one who can go with you?" she asked.

"I'm hardly a boy. Isn't it a sign of being a grown-up when you deal with things like death?" I tried to sound humorous, but I think it fell a bit flat.

"Everyone needs someone to lean on at times like this. I know what it's like to do it alone, Ben. Believe me, it isn't easy. If there's someone you could call on, contact them. I'd insist on coming with you only for needing to make sure Nathan is ok, although from the sounds of it, he won't need me for much longer. He's really taken with this place."

"He'll always need you in some way."

"You didn't have a happy childhood, did you?" she asked gently. She moved over and wrapped her arms around my shoulders and kissed the top of my head before sitting next to me.

"I did initially," I said and then went through the same sad story I'd reflected on at the cliff top.

"Oh, that's awful!" Kerry said. "She didn't try to persuade your dad to let you stay?"

"Not to my knowledge. It wasn't as if I had a good relationship with him beforehand. The shifting into a tiger just cemented his dislike of me."

"But you were a child, and it wasn't as if you did it on purpose!" Kerry said.

"Nathan is very lucky to have you. He will appreciate you even more once he has grown." Her words made me ache with longing for how a family could be. "We need to discuss when you come to leave Nathan." I had been thinking about this since I'd received the call. Kerry had to be safe, and it was driving me and my tiger to distraction knowing that we probably weren't going to be there to support and protect her.

"I think I'm going to have to look for another job. Nathan wants me to come over during school holidays. My current job wouldn't allow that. They've been really good about this leave of absence, but they have a business to run at the end of the day," Kerry said.

"I mean, the moment you leave the island. I want you to take my car. Here are the keys, plus the keys to my lodge. If you want to stay there until you decide what to do, you are more than welcome to use it. It's rent-free and near enough that you could look at the nearby towns for employment. Treat it as your own."

"No! You have already done so much!" Kerry responded.

"It's no hardship to me and it's good that the lodge will be used. I don't get up there nearly enough.

Can I ask one thing? Would you let me authorise Eddie to keep a weather eye on you? Please don't think it's in any way stalkerish. I would like to know that you're safe. Eddie can call for back-up if your brother should reappear." I wanted to be the one to protect her, but I had no doubt that Eddie could do it far better than I could when we were at a distance. That man made computers sing.

"I would rest easy knowing I had some back-up," Kerry admitted. "But I shouldn't be relying on you and your friend all the time. I feel pathetic admitting to being helpless."

I held out my hand to her. "Could I have your phone, please?" She handed it over and I undid the back. I inserted a tiny GPS chip, then handed it back to her. "That will follow you even better than Google could do. It's my chip, but I'll let Eddie know it belongs to you and he'll send a new one for me. There's also a tracker inside my car and monitoring devices in the lodge. There's no CCTV on, unless intruders come in. You will have complete privacy day-to-day; this only kicks in if you are threatened."

"Thank you, and please thank Eddie," Kerry said. "It's going to be strange you not being around. It's funny how you get used to a situation, isn't it? I feel like I've known you a lot longer than a few days."

Her words gave me some hope that she had felt as connected as I had. Perhaps I should be a little braver and not distance myself from her. "I was hoping to be here longer. Kerry, you don't need to answer this now, and we will protect you whether your answer is yes or no, but do you fancy meeting up once I've got everything at my parents sorted out and you are back on the mainland?" I decided impulsively that I couldn't go without asking her out, plus I didn't think my tiger would ever forgive me.

"Of course I would! Can we keep in touch in the meantime?" she asked. It was endearing to see the flush on her cheeks.

"Yes. Anytime. And I mean that. Don't be alone," I said.

She wrapped her arms around me and kissed me. It was tentative, but I deepened it and she responded. If my tiger could have done backflips inside me, I think he would have at that point. I'd stopped being the polite, sensible Ben and started acting like the man who was convinced he'd found his mate.

Pulling away slightly, Kerry rested her head on my forehead, giving me a slow, lazy smile. "I've wanted to do that since I first saw you when Nathan burst through the door."

"You didn't give off the impression that you wanted me anywhere near you. In fact, I seem to recall you constantly telling me to leave," I said, pecking her lips. I didn't want the kisses to stop.

"I was torn between protecting Nathan and wanting to throw myself at you," she admitted with a laugh.

"Oh, I wish you'd picked the second option," I moaned into her lips.

A cough behind us had Kerry trying to jump from my embrace, but I kept an arm around her waist and tucked her into me, part protection, part affection.

Malc was standing in the doorway, a grin on his face. "I thought I'd walk you down to the harbour, but it seems I'll be an unnecessary third."

"No, you won't," Kerry said. "Come with us." She turned to look at me, putting her hand on my shoulder. "Promise me you'll call on one of your friends to help."

"Fine," I huffed. I would ring Charlie. I know Eddie would come to me if I asked, but I wanted him to look out for Kerry. Charlie, the other partner in our new business, was American, but currently visiting his aunt in the south of England, and I knew he would respond to my appeal for company.

"Good," she said. "Now stop worrying about us and look after yourself. We have lots of dates to plan in the meantime."

I gave her one last kiss before letting her go to pick up my luggage. Lots of dates sounded good. Very good indeed. Perhaps the future wouldn't be quite so lonely after all.

Chapter 14

Kerry

I felt as if a part of me was leaving as I waved Ben off the island. How could I feel so strongly about a person who I'd known for such a short time? It was strange, but I didn't think I'd ever felt such a powerful connection, even with Dan, and I'd intended to marry him.

Turning away from the harbour as the boat sailed too far away to see anyone on board, Malc indicated that Bev was on the way towards us.

She waved in greeting. "Fancy a cuppa? The café in the town serves lovely cake."

"That would be great, thanks. Is Nathan ok?" I asked.

"He's perfectly well. Come round for the evening tonight. You'll see how well he's settling in – he's bickering with my girls as if they've been siblings since birth," Bev said, linking my arm and walking up the hill.

"Oh no! I'll have a word with him!" I was mortified at her words.

"You'll do nothing of the sort," she responded with a gentle squeeze. "He's got to be one of the family or he won't settle properly. It's lovely to see. I'd hoped it would happen, and I'm pleased as punch that it's happened so soon. It means the right family was chosen for him, which I'm going to take full credit for, obviously."

"Who decided?" I asked, knowing I hadn't asked nearly enough questions when we'd first arrived. I was just so relieved at getting here; the set-up on the island had seemed secondary in importance.

"The committee. When you made contact, there were discussions about Nathan, including his background and what we thought would be best for him. It isn't the first time someone has a similar story to Nathan and they've come to live with us. Many of the families have sons and daughters who aren't their birth children, but you wouldn't know it unless it was pointed out to you. We thought that with Nathan being an only child, it would be better for him to be the eldest in a family. They have a bit more authority over the younger children."

"But what about your daughter? She's gone from being the eldest to being the middle child? Does she not feel annoyed about the change? I'm not sure my brother would have coped with a similar situation," I said about Neil. I kept forcing down my own feelings of sadness at losing Nathan and being replaced by another family who could offer him so much. I constantly reminded myself that my feelings were selfish.

"She's still the eldest daughter. It sounds very old-fashioned, but shifter communities are used to having a hierarchy and for that to change from time to time," Bev said.

"From the little I know of the shifter world, I can understand that happening and being accepted in groups of, say, wolves, but with your community, you are all different animals. Ben said he was a lone animal, so what if lots of you chose to have a lone animal as your dominant one?"

"I'm as human as you are," Bev said. "But it's like anyone, I suppose, it's safety in numbers. This group is a minority group of a minority group, so although there can be a few spats now and again, most of us realise that there is a benefit in us living together. I think it helps that there isn't officially an alpha male either. It's very much committee led, which can have its own problems, but at least there aren't challenges for the top spot."

"I presumed you were a shifter," I admitted. "Is it strange leaving the human world behind?" I couldn't help but ask the question, and I blushed at her response.

"As I'm guessing that query comes from a more personal position than just general curiosity, I think we should settle in first, order our cake and then I'll tell you what I think is useful."

Glad of the distraction of being seated at a table and then ordering from the surprisingly wide array of cakes on offer, I was able to stop myself from blushing at Bev's words. The café was full and everyone acknowledged us. I had never been in a place where everyone seemed so friendly. A few people came over and introduced themselves to me, typically those with children who would be at school with Nathan. It was very kind of them to express that they were looking forward to getting to know both of us.

"They cater for the shifter appetite," she explained as I stared at the delicious-looking cakes.

"It's true when they say life is unfair," I smiled at her. "I'd love to be able to eat cake without consequences."

"Me too. Malc can be a beast when he's in a tormenting mood. I have sometimes banned him and the girls from the house when they are in full can't eat enough mode," she laughed.

I was once again assured that Nathan would love being with them; they seemed like such a well-rounded, fun family.

When we had our own large slices of cake, Bev smiled at me. "Are you aware of fated mates?" she asked.

"Fated mates? I've heard of mates and how shifters mate for life. Some of that very recently; I don't know whether that thought is scary or quite appealing," I admitted. Bev and Malc had obviously seen the attraction I had towards Ben and his towards me.

"Shifters can mate and they do for life, but the lucky ones meet with their fated mates. I'm Malc's," Bev explained.

"How can you tell the difference?"

"It's almost a compulsion to touch them, to be with them. It sounds corny, but like a moth to a flame, it's what we know as love at first sight," Bev said.

"It happened so quickly," I admitted.

"It does," she smiled at me. "You are very lucky to have found him. Shifters are the most loyal, loving protectors you could wish to find. Think Mr Darcy on steroids."

"Wouldn't steroids make him angry?" I laughed.

"Ok, Mr Darcy with primal feelings and you as the centre of his world."

"I'm sold!"

"That's good that you've accepted who he is. Many human men and women struggle against their urges towards shifters. Although, to be fair, some shifters do too. They don't want to risk not producing shifter babies, for it's no guarantee that they will have babies who can shift if they mate with a human."

"Can we stop talking about babies?" I groaned. "I've only just met him. I'm still trying to process the large tiger aspect, never mind the fated mates part."

Bev laughed. "That you aren't running back to the hills already is a good start."

"No. I don't want to do that," I admitted.

"I know exactly what you're feeling. There's no point in fighting it – you're doomed," Bev grinned at me.

"I feel I need more cake," I responded, but the butterflies of anticipation in my stomach swirled in excitement at some sort of future with Ben. It was crazy, but felt so right, I had to believe Bev's words. I had wanted to touch Ben since the moment I'd seen him; it had been an almost primal reaction to his animal, I suppose. I took a mouthful of delicious cream sponge. It was divine and I was able to pretend I was enjoying the cake while thoughts of Ben ran through my mind. I wanted to be with him, and the thought of it being for life didn't scare me at all. In fact, it put a smile on my face.

"Good cake?" Bev asked.

"The best," I responded happily, and he was – the best man I'd ever met.

*

The day I was going to leave Nathan was always going to be hard. I'd promised I'd return as often as I could until he could safely come to the mainland, but it was still heartbreaking to leave him on the harbour side.

I knew he would be well. The week I'd spent on the island had convinced me that even if Viv had been alive, this was the perfect place for him to be. He was around people who understood him like we couldn't, no matter how much we wished we could.

We'd hugged and cried for most of the previous day, even though it was right for me to leave. I was a distraction to him; however much Malc and Bev included me in their home life, which they did every day, I was an outsider and Nathan wouldn't completely immerse himself in his new life until I'd left.

I'd thanked Bev and Malc a hundred times or more, until they both banned me from saying another word if the sentence contained 'I can never' and 'thank you'.

Waving at the harbour until I couldn't see Nathan any longer, I turned to watch for the shore of the mainland.

It had been a strange week; Ben had been in touch by text, but nothing else. I'd presumed there would be phone calls, but then had cursed myself when there hadn't been. Of course he had things to do and he might not feel like talking when he was dealing with the loss of his mother, I had berated myself. I took comfort in knowing that his friend had been there for the first two days when he'd first returned home, but I couldn't shake the feeling that Ben was holding something back from our brief text conversations.

The skipper of the boat helped me into the dinghy and we started the short journey to the harbour. It was as quiet as it had been when we'd left it.

"Just let whoever's on duty know that you're taking the car from the shed," the skipper instructed as he helped me onto land once more. "Or you'll probably get an animal chasing you to wherever you're going, thinking you've stolen the car!"

I smiled at him. "They've got the spare keys anyway, so I need to pop in and collect those," I said. "I know Ben was going to tell them I would be taking the car." Ben had got a lift from the harbour to the airport at Inverness from one of the community who lived on the mainland. It was a journey of a few hours, and it just showed how decent and quick to help these people were.

"Ah, ok. Well, good luck to you. We'll probably see you in the school holidays, but you can come over whenever you want; we're always at the ready," he said, climbing back into the dinghy and casting off the rope.

"Thank you, I appreciate that," I said.

I waited until the dinghy had set off safely and then walked into the ferry building. There was only one man on duty; it wasn't the most thriving of harbours.

"Hello, I'm Kerry. I'm here to collect Ben Wilson's car."

"Yes, I've been waiting for you. Malc told me you'd be coming with the boat today," the man behind the counter said. "The spare keys are actually in the car. I turned over the engine for you this morning. Have you far to go?"

"No. Not too far today," I admitted. I'd decided to take Ben up on his offer of staying at the lodge. I know Neil knew where it was, but he also knew where I lived, and at home, I didn't have as much protection as I would have at Ben's place. For my first few days back on the mainland, I wanted to build up to facing my brother again, for I knew it was inevitable that he'd seek me out.

"That's good. It can be strange coming back to the busy roads after a spell on the island. Best to break yourself in gently. Malc said I should warn you to keep your wits about you – there have been a few strangers driving down to the harbour. It could be completely unconnected to your situation, but Malc thought it best to mention."

My blood ran cold at the thought that Neil had managed to track me here. "You think they were looking for Nathan?"

"Sometimes we get people who are lost, or who are just exploring the area, so it could be innocent, but they didn't appear to be tourists. Just be careful."

"Yes, I will," I said.

Walking out the door, I started to cross the large concrete area where the cars were parked before they caught the ferry to the other islands. I turned when I heard a car coming into the harbour area at speed. Seeing a large black 4x4, I faltered. It wasn't the car I'd seen Neil in, but I knew without doubt that it was him.

Frozen to the spot, I was jolted out of my stupor by the man from the ferry terminal running out of the building. "Kerry! Get to the car!" he shouted at me.

"It's no use; I won't be able to outrun him," I admitted. It had been Ben who had dodged Neil last time. I wouldn't be able to undertake the same sort of car chase without crashing, and I didn't have Eddie having set up a scheme to get me to safety – it had taken him time to get organised.

The harbour man ran away from the door of the ferry building towards the shed containing Ben's car. My mind was reeling as to how I could convince Neil once and for all that it was time to give up his cause.

The large car squealed to a halt a few feet away from me, and I felt my heart sink when not only Neil, but two other men got out of the car. These weren't the goons he'd been with before; they looked just as beefy, but there was something else about them, an air of real danger, which made me take an involuntary step back.

"Stay where you are!" one of the men spat, pointing a pistol at my middle.

Having never had a gun pointed at me before, I wasn't surprised that my reaction was to go completely cold and my knees to wobble. Having to force myself to breathe and not just pass out, I tried to focus on something other than the gun, which was nearly impossible.

Neil walked around the front of the car and joined his two buddies. He looked pleased with himself. "It's time to stop messing around, Kerry," he started. "My two friends here are tired of waiting for Nathan."

"You were going to hand him over to men who think it's acceptable to wave guns around?" I asked.

"They were the highest bidders." He shrugged.

"I didn't think my opinion of you could get any lower, but apparently I was wrong," I spat at him.

"Enough of this family reunion. We want the boy," the man with the gun said to us both. His accent was Eastern European, and I was terrified to think who wanted Nathan so badly that they were prepared to go to these lengths.

I can't say I've ever considered myself a brave person, but I knew this was the time to stop this, even if it meant losing my life. I sent up a silent apology to Ben, hoping that he could forgive me for what I was going to say next. I knew he would understand in the long term that I had to do this for Nathan's safety.

"You obviously know about shifters and magic," I started, looking at the two men. "Then you will know I am not lying when I say that Nathan has gone. He is being protected by strong magic, which you will never overcome. It is time to give this chase up; you've lost. There is no way you could reach him now."

I didn't need to be a body language expert to know that I'd really upset all three of them with my words, and I mean *really* upset them.

The two strangers babbled in their language whilst Neil took a step towards me. "You stupid bitch!" he snarled. "Have you any idea who you're dealing with here? They aren't going to give up so easily. You'd better warn your shifter buddies, because if these two start on them, they'll all be tortured."

"You were going to give your own nephew up to be tortured?" I couldn't believe – even after all that had happened – that he could be so evil.

Before Neil had a chance to reply, the man with the gun spoke. "This changes the situation. We were promised the boy; he has not been delivered as promised. Our agreement is at an end."

Neil swung around to face them. "You can't renege on the deal! I've brought you as close as I can get you to him. She is the key," he cried out.

"You are right. We'll get the boy through her. You are now surplus to our needs."

Before Neil or I could process the words, the gun was turned towards Neil, and two bullets were fired into his chest in quick succession.

I screamed and stumbled away from the men as my brother's body flew backwards with the force of the bullets. He landed heavily on the ground and I knew with only a glance at him that he'd been dead before he hit the concrete.

"Now, come. You are with us and going to tell us where your nephew is. Believe me when I say there is more than one way to die. Before we have finished with you, you will realise that we were kind to your brother."

I just felt hot all over and a buzzing was in my ears. I fought to keep from fainting. If I passed out, there would be no chance of escape, although I could have laughed at my train of thought – there was no way I could get away from them. As if to confirm my own thoughts, the gunman shot at the concrete, just in front of my feet, sending shards of the grey material scattering up.

"Come on!" he snarled.

It was the final straw for me. I did what every average person would do in the same circumstances – I crouched over, hand to my stomach, and started to vomit.

I could tell that they were cursing me in their native tongue, but thankfully, neither tried to approach me. They probably didn't want their nice, clean car to get messed up. Retching while I tried to think wasn't a good combination, but as the convulsions started to ease, I saw that they were distracted by something behind me.

Looking at them from my crouched position, they were looking at the sky behind me. Risking a glance behind, I could understand why they were stunned. The sky seemed full of birds. At first, I thought it was a flock of seagulls, but as they got closer, I could see they were far larger than any seagull I'd ever seen.

There must have been dozens, and they had created a large black cloud. One of the men glanced at me and I retched again, although there was nothing left in my stomach. I had a feeling about the birds and I wanted to delay being forced to get into the car.

It seemed my hunch was correct, because the birds started to dive towards us. The gunman began to shoot at the birds, but he'd already shot two rounds into Neil, so he was soon out of ammunition. I was glad to see that it didn't look as if he'd hit any of them as they all continued towards us.

Managing to shuffle backwards a little, I was able to put a little bit of distance between myself and the men, just at the time that the birds started to attack.

Guns were forgotten while the men tried to protect their faces against the onslaught. It was like something out of a Hitchcock film, only these were exceptionally large birds of prey. They swooped in for attack after attack, the men unable to withstand the constant barrage, falling to their knees, screaming out in pain.

Behind me came the roar of an engine, and Ben's car was driven towards me. The man from the ferry terminal jumped out of the driver's seat and threw my luggage into the car.

"Get in and get away from here!" he yelled at me.

"Did you bring them here?" I asked, but I was moving to the driver's side as I spoke.

"Yes. Now leave and forget about this."

"Thank you for your help," I said, scrambling in.

"We don't take kindly to those who threaten our safety – now go!" he shouted, slamming the door on me.

I didn't need to be told twice. Pushing my foot on the accelerator, I forced myself not to look at the horrific scene in the rear-view mirror. I would have nightmares enough after today.

Chapter 15

Ben

Knocking on my old home, a myriad of emotions pulsed through my body until my father opened the door, then I stiffened, ready for anything. He didn't acknowledge me, just turned on his heel and walked down the hallway. The fact that he hadn't slammed the door in my face was a positive, I supposed, as I followed him into the house.

Returning to this house was strange; I hadn't been back in years and it wasn't a pleasant feeling which washed over me as I walked into the kitchen. Nothing had changed. Mum's apron still hung on the peg set immediately as you walked into the room. Her rubber gloves were threaded through the drawer handle as they always were. It was as if she'd just popped out for a moment. I could still smell her scent in the house, which caused my stomach to churn. It was at times like these when having a heightened sense of smell wasn't a good thing.

Dad opened a kitchen drawer, pulled out a set of keys and threw them to me. "These are for your grandmother's house and here. I'll be out all day tomorrow. It's too late for you to start now, so you can come and go as you please from first thing in the morning. The funeral is on Monday; there isn't going to be a wake afterwards." There was absolutely no emotion there at all. I couldn't believe how anyone could be so callous.

Fuming inside, I knew he would sense my anger, but I wasn't giving him the pleasure of saying what I was thinking. No way was I going to play into his hands like I had in the past. Then I'd been an impetuous teenager; now I was a man fully in control of my emotions.

"A copy of her will is here," he continued. "Plus the legal documents to do with your grandmother's house. I've put the rest of her belongings in your old room, and you can check the other rooms to see if I've missed anything. But stay out of my bedroom. There's nothing in there for you, and I don't want your scent in that room. It'll be bad enough until I can purge it from the rest of the house."

"I've got a friend coming over to help." I was glad I'd taken Kerry's advice and asked Charlie to join me for a couple of days. He was driving up from Hampshire today, so he could help out tomorrow before returning to his aunt.

"Is he like you?" Dad sneered.

"Does it matter as long as it means I will get her stuff emptied in half the time?"

"I suppose not."

We stood staring at one another in silence. There really was nothing connecting us at all. I turned away from him, hating that I broke eye contact first. I knew how he worked – he would see that as a victory, but I was beyond caring at this point.

"Thanks, *Dad*," I said sarcastically, emphasising the word.

"Let's get one thing straight. I am not your father, thank God! Now get out of my house."

*

I'd been shocked at his words and part of me had not believed him, but he had included papers within my mum's legal documents which proved that I wasn't his son. Talk about relief! I'd been haunted for years that I had his genes running through me and hated that I might turn out to be as nasty and vindictive as he was. At least I no longer had that worry.

Grandma's house was nothing like it had been when I'd lived at home. She'd died a few years ago and Mum had spent her time refurbishing the house and was about to let it out to tenants. From Mum's will, it now belonged to me.

There was no way I could keep the house. I'd had happy times at Grandma's, but this house no longer had any traces of her or Mum in it, so I would be selling the property. The quicker I could sever all connections to this village now that Mum had gone, the better.

When Charlie arrived, I updated him about everything that had happened, as we sat enjoying a couple of beers.

"Wow. I suppose it makes sense him not being your father. I've never known two people less alike than you two, plus it explains the tiger/wolf mix."

"Doesn't it just," I said wryly. "I think I always suspected, but was afraid it was more of a hope on my part that I wasn't related to him."

"What are you going to do?" Charlie asked.

"I don't suppose there's a lot I can do. We're talking over thirty years ago, and the person who could supply the information is about to be buried," I said. "They got a duplicate birth certificate and falsified the details on it."

"It probably happens more than we know." Charlie shrugged. "More importantly, I can stay until after your mom's funeral if you need me to."

It always made me smile that Charlie had spent so much time in England as he was growing up and then years abroad in the military, so his American accent was only slight. Yet, he would sometimes use an American word and I'd be reminded he wasn't a native of England, even though it felt like he was. He couldn't have been closer to me if we were brothers.

"Thanks, but I think it's best if the villagers only see one tiger shifter. They might get their stakes and pick axes out if they know there's two of us," I said. The funeral would be difficult, but it was something I wasn't going to put Charlie through; he was helping enough just by being here for the day.

"It is like a village out of the dark ages," he said, swigging back his beer. "I don't know how you stood it until university."

We had met at university and had been inseparable, along with Eddie. The miles separating us since we'd left hadn't made the slightest dent in our friendship, and it was one of the reasons we were keen to work together; only Charlie's deployment had delayed things a little.

"I had little choice. No money means limited options," I admitted. "You know as well as any of us that parents aren't perfect. How is your Aunt Jean?" I asked of the person who had been the constant in Charlie's life.

"She's her same scary self," he answered with a laugh. "She's formidable and misses absolutely nothing."

"So, you're on your best behaviour down there?"

"I am, but I'd like not to be," he admitted.

"Oh, tell me more." I was happy for the subject change; it would help take my mind off what I needed to do tomorrow.

"I've met a woman who's complicated, but I think she could be the one – no, she is the one," Charlie admitted with a slight blush, which is something when you considered he was over six feet in height, almost as wide as tall, muscled and heavily tattooed. He appeared to be the person least likely to blush, but here he was turning pink.

"Your fated mate?"

"The way both my tiger and I reacted towards her, yes," he admitted.

"Wow. That's amazing." His words immediately had me wanting to tell him of Kerry, but this wasn't about me. Charlie had never had a serious relationship in his life. To go from casual flings to his fated mate was something huge.

"It's complicated," he grimaced.

"Isn't it always?" I smiled. "Is she a shifter?"

"No. I'd thought there was a real chance of being involved with something good, but in my own usual way, I've managed to mess it up spectacularly. She had a lot of secrets, and I wasn't patient enough to wait until she told me, and then she found out. Your call came at just the right time to give us a little space. I'm hoping she's calmed down a little when I return." He smiled, but I could see he was worried that he'd messed up.

"Take it slowly," I advised. "The shifter part can be hard enough to accept, without throwing a tiger in the mix. Add fated mates into it and she might just self-combust."

Charlie laughed. "I'm going to have to succeed because I can't live without her. I know that already. It's not going to be easy – I've enough issues without adding hers to the mix, but I have to try and overcome them, because I can't stand the thought of living without her."

We fell silent for a while. To know your fated mate, but not be able to mate with them, had sent more than one shifter over the edge. It wasn't a good situation to be in, and I hoped that Charlie could sort it out with this woman he'd found. It was the same hope I had for myself.

"I wish you all the luck in the world, pal," I said. "If there's anything I can do to help, just let me know."

"Thanks. I think it might be a case of patience, which you know I'm not good at," Charlie grinned.

"Err, no. Not one of your fortes."

*

We entered Mum's old house after I received a text saying the house was empty. I hadn't replied to the message, just gone straight to the house. The quicker I could get this over and done with, the better.

Walking into my old room, it was clear that before having Mum's things put in it, nothing had changed since I'd left. Strange really, when you think I hadn't been wanted, but it didn't matter now. It couldn't change feelings or what had happened at this point. Mum's actions still hurt me, more so now that I knew there was a reason for her husband's hatred of me. I could no longer call him Dad; he'd made that perfectly clear, and I didn't want to give him the respect of the title.

Boxes and suitcases were piled haphazardly around the room, and papers littered the bed. Looking around the space, I let out a huff of breath. "I don't want to sort all this here. It's going to take days and I want to be in this place as little as he wants me here. You ok with carrying everything to Grandma's house?" The houses were only a few doors apart so it wouldn't be a major trek between the two houses, but there would be a lot of trips.

"I'm here to do whatever you want," Charlie said, picking up a couple of boxes nearest to him.

We spent the next couple of hours moving everything, and when my old bedroom was empty, I did a quick check through the rest of the house. I couldn't find anything which had been overlooked, so I locked the front door and posted the house keys through the letterbox. Sending a text to say I'd finished, I turned my back on the house and walked away.

Charlie stood, hands on hips, surveying the lounge, which we stood at the edge of. "I can stay a bit longer," he said. "This is going to take you ages."

"I know, but it will give me something to do," I admitted. "I'm better keeping busy, and I'll have to wait around until the estate agents have been and started the process of getting this place on the market."

"If you're sure," Charlie said. "It's daunting to me and it's not my responsibility. I don't like leaving you so soon."

"I'm sort of hoping it gives me some clues about her," I said. "I never understood the decisions she made and it caused a breach between us. Having found out that Richard isn't my father, I'm even more confused. Perhaps this lot will give me some answers."

"I hope so for your sake," Charlie said. "Right, let's have something substantial to eat before I set off back to the lovely Lizzy."

After eating enough to feed an army, Charlie set off back to Hampshire. His visit had been brief, but I was glad of it; the task ahead was not as daunting now that everything was in Grandma's house. Sitting down on the floor, I started to go through the first box.

Two hours later, there was a shard of light at the end of the tunnel. I sorted out all Mum's clothing, and although it was a weird thing to do, I just closed my mind to it and got on with the task. Arranging for a charity shop to come and collect everything I was getting rid of was the most effective way of dealing with it, which I would do once they opened the following week.

Surprisingly, sorting through her paperwork was harder. I had to do it in stages – I wasn't as immune to grief as I thought I was, and as the waves of sorrow washed over me, I would stop and try to get my feelings under control before starting on the grim task once more.

*

Monday dawned grey and dreary; perfect for a funeral, some would say. Thankfully, the funeral was early. I'd have lost my nerve about attending if I'd had to hang around all day for it.

Entering the church was always going to be difficult. I'd been sent a text to say it was expected that I would follow the coffin in, pretending that we were still a respectable family, but it meant that everyone was already seated. The murmur of whispering which went along the pews would have been funny if it hadn't been so pathetic. Whether or not I would return for the funeral had obviously caused some speculation.

The service was short, with no eulogies allowed. It was explained away as a wish of my mother's. I didn't believe it for a second. People followed the entourage to the graveside, and all too soon, the deed was done. The mourners didn't hang around; quite a few acknowledged Richard, but no one came near me. I was glad. I didn't want false platitudes at this point.

About to turn away, I heard my name being called quietly, so as not to draw the attention of any of the few still lingering in the graveyard. Looking back, I thought I'd recognised the woman as an old friend of my mother's. I remembered her spending quite a bit of time in our house as I'd grown up.

"I'm glad you came," she said as she approached me.

"Not sure whether the rest of the village would agree with you," I said, indicating that although no one was approaching us, quite a few people were looking over at us in disgust. It seemed the wolf pack didn't even like a tiger-shifter visiting their area.

"Small-minded dogs, that's all they are," she said with a scowl at the nearest people to us.

I didn't comment that she was also a wolf shifter. "How are you, Mrs Ward?"

"Older, wiser, not as stupid as my neighbours," she answered. "Take a walk with me."

I followed her lead, walking deeper into the graveyard which surrounded the church, away from prying eyes. She stopped at a monument to the deceased members of her own family.

"This is where we all end up," she said. "We should make sure we sort out our lives and our secrets before we pass."

"You know about the lie of who my father is then?"

"Yes, we were friends from school. There was nothing we didn't share, although I can't say I agreed with some of her decisions," Mrs Ward acknowledged. "And it's too late for her to sort them out. She always did try to avoid confrontation."

"She picked the wrong husband then," I said dryly. "There was nothing but arguments in our house."

"I know, but the reality was that she had little choice. You were on the way, and she had already been promised to Richard; there was a hasty marriage. Richard said he would bring you up as his own if it meant he had your mother, but then he reneged and punished her and you," Mrs Ward said. "In some ways, I think he was afraid of you when it was discovered what you were. A tiger is a far stronger beast than a wolf, after all."

"I wouldn't have made life difficult for anyone," I said.

"No, but when you are a nasty man to start with, you look for any way of gaining the upper hand. Having you driven out of the village was genius on his part – he could use it against her forever."

"Why did she choose him over me? Why didn't she leave?" As I'd said to Kerry, if the partner is abusive, divorces are allowed.

"I think she considered it her punishment." Mrs Ward shrugged. "I never understood it and tried to persuade her to leave on numerous occasions. I would have supported her financially if she'd gone. When your grandma died, I thought she would sell the house and use the money to get away, but I think by that time it was almost second nature to her to be with him."

"I don't think I'll ever understand."

"No."

"Do you know who my real father is? Does he know about me?"

"I know he was a tiger shifter and I know he was the love of your mother's life, her fated mate, but she let him go because of fear of what telling her family would cause, when they had already arranged her marriage to Richard."

"She really didn't like conflict if she could let her true mate go," I said.

"It was a different time then and she was human," Mrs Ward said. "I'm not excusing her actions, but she might as well have been born to a shifter family; her father was so domineering. Whatever he said went without question, or there would be consequences. She did regret not supporting you, though. Losing you was like losing her mate all over again."

"Yet, she let it happen." I know I sounded bitter, but I was. No point in hiding it at this stage.

"Yes, she did. I've got something for you." Reaching into her handbag, she pulled out a large, thick envelope. "Do her one last service and read what's in here. There are details about your father. Whether or not you want to do anything with them, that's up to you. Good luck to you, Ben. You've turned into a fine man and she was so proud of you."

Mrs Ward's words made tears spring to my eyes, something which hadn't happened during the funeral. I took the envelope from her and tucked it under my arm. "I will look through everything."

"I don't know if your father knew about you or not," she said. "It might say in those papers. I haven't looked at them. Your mum gave them to me for safekeeping and I honoured the promise I gave her."

"Thank you."

"You're welcome, Ben. I hope you can find a family who will appreciate you as you should be."

I immediately thought of Kerry and of how much I'd missed her. I'd purposely not bombarded her with messages, even though I'd been desperate to over the last few days. I'd wanted to hear her voice, but I was aware how deep my feelings were for her and I didn't want to frighten her off when she had so much else going on. Humans sometimes didn't understand the fated mates thing, and although she'd asked questions, it didn't mean she was prepared to take the step, whereas I was sure it was a step I was ready to take. The more time we were apart, the more I was coming to realise that I really needed her, to be near her and to be able to openly adore her. For someone who had longed for but been terrified of commitment, it was a scary position to be in.

Chapter 16

Kerry

I've no idea how I didn't get stopped, crash the car, or pull over in a wobbly heap and cry, but somehow I managed to focus, drive to Aviemore and stop at a supermarket, stocking up on as much food as I could fit in a trolley. I drove to Ben's lodge, constantly checking to make sure I wasn't being followed. Unloading all the food I'd bought, I then drove the car back to Aviemore and parked at the station. I tried to avoid a CCTV camera that could be used to track my location and started on the long journey back to the lodge.

It took nearly five hours of walking, avoiding main roads and trying not to look like the towny I was. I could have made the journey quicker, but I wanted to avoid anyone being able to track me. I knew Ben's friend Eddie could and I'd even thought of contacting him for help, but I couldn't rely on them for my protection, not with the brutal people I was now dealing with. It could mean they were put in danger by association and I couldn't have that on my conscience.

Exhausted, cold and wet, I forced myself to circle the lodge, checking that there was no sign of anyone. I was no expert in tracking anything, but I did what I could until I was as happy as I could be that whoever had been with Neil hadn't escaped from the attack they faced, or followed me.

Locking the door behind me as soon as I entered the lodge, I dragged a table over and set it against the door. I had toyed with the idea of getting into my own car, which was still parked outside Ben's lodge, and driving home, but they could easily trace my home address. Here, there was the slight chance of my being safe. I hoped.

Taking a hot shower, I poured myself a large glass of wine. I wasn't usually one who drank alone, but my shaking hands convinced me that I needed the courage boost the alcohol would bring.

Switching the television on, I went straight to the news channels to see if anything had been reported about what had happened at the ferry terminal, but there was nothing. Flicking through all the channels, I couldn't believe that something like that would happen and not make the news.

There was at least one dead person and two badly injured men, if the screams were anything to go by. I still shuddered at the memory. I knew I would be having nightmares about that alone.

Neil was dead. I didn't know whether to feel relief, grief or just plain numbness at the thought. No, I didn't wish my brother dead, but it meant the chase was over, yet it didn't feel so quite yet. Those men he'd been with were no nonsense, dedicated to getting what they wanted, and that's what still had me shaking after my second glass of wine.

My mobile ringing interrupted my musings. It was Malc's number and I answered immediately.

"Hello. Is everything ok with Nathan?" I asked.

"Yes, no need to worry. I just wanted to check in that you were ok after today," Malc said. His voice was as calm as always and I relaxed when I heard it. Being alone had increased my worry and paranoia.

"Malc, there's nothing on the news about what happened, even the local news."

"No. There won't be."

"My brother died and a flock of birds attacked men."

"And the authorities don't want to make any more of the fact that some members of the human world threatened the shifter world today. Don't worry, no one gets away with anything if laws have been broken, but it would do neither side any good to create further antagonism," Malc said.

"Those birds..."

"Yes, Joe had put a call in the moment your brother came down to the terminal. We responded to that call."

I'd known it was them who had flown across – there was no possibility that birds could act in such a focused way without attacking me too, if it had been a natural phenomenon. "But you hurt two men and you said it was rare for shifters to turn into birds," I said weakly.

"Rare but not impossible. We did hurt them and we have to deal with that. They had murdered another in cold blood, and although it doesn't make it right, be under no illusion, you would have ended the same way as your brother and we would have been attacked in some way. It couldn't be allowed, Kerry. These people are intent on hurting some of our community; we can't stand back and let that happen," Malc said. "I know this is hard to understand, but we live with threats every day. This is new to you, but believe me, we are not some vigilante group. We've been working with the police all day, which is why I haven't been able to contact you until now."

"I'm sorry for being so negative," I said.

"Don't be; it's perfectly natural. Your brother's body has been taken to the mainland hospital. I've given the police your telephone number, but I've told them I've no idea where you are and I don't want to know."

It was a strange comment for Malc to make and I was immediately on the alert. "What are you telling me, Malc?"

"There was a third in the car," he said gently. "After the two men on the harbour side had been incapacitated, there was a lot of activity and none of us thought to check the vehicle. He managed to get away."

"Oh God."

"It was some time after you'd left. I don't think he can have followed you."

"I was checking behind me the whole time I was driving and never saw anything," I admitted.

"He's probably returned to whoever they're working for and forgotten about you," Malc assured me.

"Is Nathan safe?" It was nice of Malc to try to reassure me, but we both knew he was wrong. I couldn't criticise him for it; I knew he was trying his best to offer me some little spark of relief from everything which was going on.

"Yes. He's perfectly safe while he's with us, I promise you that. You've seen how we work together to protect each other. I just wanted to let you know so that you can be on the alert. Have you let Ben know about what happened?"

"No. He's got enough on his plate at the moment," I answered. I didn't want to admit that apart from texting each other, we hadn't spoken since Ben had left the island. I still had the feeling that something had happened since he'd arrived home, and although I wanted to help if I could, little could be done if he didn't confide in me. I hoped that it wasn't just him changing his mind about what we'd shared on the island.

"I think he would want to know," Malc said.

"I'll tell him when he rings." If ever he rings, I said silently.

"Just make sure you take care of yourself and be a bit more aware of your surroundings and the people you come into contact with until we know if the threat has passed."

"I will. Thanks for your concern," I said.

"Whenever you want to come over here, just let us know. You're always welcome," he assured me.

"I might leave it for a little while to let everything die down," I admitted. I didn't mention that it was going to be quite a while before I left this cabin.

"Ok, whatever is best for you. If there is a problem, Kerry, let the police know first and then contact us. We do have a network of support on the mainland."

"You've done so much for us already," I said, hating that I felt weak and feeble, but until today, I hadn't realised just how determined people could be when they wanted something badly enough.

"That's because you're part of the family now. I'm sorry to break it to you, but there's no escape – we look after our own and those closest to them," Malc said. There was a smile in his voice and my lips twitched in response.

"Cheers, Malc. Now go and have a beer; you've been a superhero for long enough."

"Oh, the beer is in the fridge, don't worry."

"Please pass my thanks on to everyone. Bye, Malc," I said, ending the call.

I wedged the cork back in the top of the wine bottle. There was a third man and he was on the loose. Any relaxing effects the wine had been having had immediately disappeared at Malc's words. Suddenly, the cabin felt claustrophobic and very restricting. I started to panic before I reminded myself – this was ridiculous; I needed to stay focused and be prepared.

Searching through the cabin, the only weapon I could find was a kitchen knife. I don't suppose a person needed many weapons when you had claws you could rip out someone's throat with and an extremely large set of scary teeth. Getting the largest knife out of the drawer, I placed it on the table next to where I was seated.

It was going to be a long night.

*

As the days progressed, I became a little surer that I wouldn't be attacked while in the lodge. I'd heard a couple of vehicles, but I'd closed the curtains so that I could peep outside when I needed to, and the cars only went to the other lodges. Two families had come up for a few days and their presence had been a comfort.

I'd considered leaving the lodge, but although it was approaching the time when I was going to have to, or starve to death, I wasn't quite ready for it.

Malc had sent a text every day asking how I was doing, which I was grateful for, as each time he offered help if I needed it.

I'd spoken to Nathan a few times, and he was full of what he was doing and discovering about his talent. It made all the worry and the sleepless nights worth it to hear the excitement in his voice. I never mentioned what had happened with Neil and nor did he. I wondered if he knew anything, but presumed that he wouldn't have been told what had happened. There was no point in worrying him when there was nothing that could be done.

The police had contacted me about Neil, but he had already been identified. I didn't ask who by and they didn't need anything from me once I'd given the details of an undertaker. They said there was going to be an investigation, as there would be with every murder, but I wasn't needed for anything. Again, I wondered what they'd been told and if I was being excused because of being connected to the shifter world. I knew without a doubt that, in normal circumstances, they would want to speak to me. It was almost as if they wanted me as far away from the enquiry as possible and I was glad of it.

Going into a police station would make me vulnerable if someone was watching from the outside. After all, it was a direct connection through Neil to me and through me to Nathan.

A week after I'd moved into the lodge, I finally ran out of milk. It seems petty, but I didn't realise the need I have for numerous cups of tea in a day, so this was a disaster. I had weighed up whether or not I wanted to travel back to the supermarket to replenish stock, but decided it was foolish. I couldn't hide away forever; I'd not been outside for a whole seven days, and I probably looked like a vampire. It was time to put the knife away, clear up the lodge and go home. I had to return to normality at some point.

Deciding what I was going to do was a wake-up call. With renewed energy, I scrubbed the lodge and left everything as I'd found it, if not better. I'd not heard from Ben for a full day, so I was coming to the conclusion that whatever spark we'd shared was only there for him whilst he was in my company. A shame, as I still ached for him, but that was life and we didn't always get what we wanted.

Gathering my luggage near the door, I left Ben's car keys on the kitchen worktop and turned to leave.

A loud knocking had me reaching for the knife I'd so confidently put away just a few hours before. There was a pause and I tried to hold my breath.

"Kerry, open the door!" Ben's voice sounded from the outside.

Chapter 17

Ben

Sorting through Mum's possessions was both cathartic and nostalgic. Getting rid of clothing and the items that were hers but not personal to her was relatively easy to deal with, as all of it went to the charity shop during the days after the funeral. It was when I started sorting through the boxes that contained the things she'd kept because they were important to her that I found myself struggling with emotions.

I couldn't believe how many of my things she'd saved: all the cards I'd ever sent her at birthdays, Mother's Days and Christmas; any pictures I'd drawn when young, none of which I could remember. It was bittersweet looking through them, because I wanted to ask her so many questions and now it was too late. Looking back over the messages I'd written in the cards, it was emotional to see how full of love and adoration for her I'd been as a boy.

Of course, that was before she turned away from me when I really needed her support.

Eventually, all that was left to go through was the thick envelope which Mrs Ward had given me at the funeral. I hadn't opened it, just left it on the kitchen worktop and glared at it every time I walked past.

Cursing my inability to face what it contained, I ripped it open, and inside were several documents.

Two bank books caught my eye. I didn't even realise people still had bank books; I thought everything was done with cards or online. I was even more surprised when I opened them. They were in my name and contained, between the two of them, just over half a million pounds. Sitting down heavily on one of the breakfast bar stools, I rubbed my hand through my hair as I gazed at the books. Half a million pounds in my name.

I wasn't exactly poor; I was single and, until recently, had worked as a police inspector, so I had a steady income every month, but this was on another level. It was change your life money, or at least make it extremely comfortable from now on.

There was a birth certificate, which was mine, but I had my own. Only there was one significant difference with this certificate: it had the name Alexander Benjamin Ratchford written in the box for the father's name. Mum had always said I'd been named after a family member, but never who. It was obviously after my real father, but that didn't explain how another birth certificate had been produced with false details on it. Letting out a breath, I realised I wasn't Ben Wilson at all, I was Ben Ratchford. I wasn't sure if I wanted to take that name on, even though I disliked with a passion the man who I'd thought of as my father.

The deeds of my grandma's house were also included, and finally, a letter. Opening it up, I started to read, wondering just what surprises this would have in store.

My dearest Ben,

If you have received this, then I am gone without reaching out to you and fixing what probably cannot be fixed. Oh my darling boy, I have loved you so much and hurt you in ways a mother should never hurt her child.

I am not going to ask for your forgiveness because it should never be given, nor am I looking to excuse my behaviour, but I wanted you to know that the decisions were made to try and protect you, beyond the hurt you had to endure.

I loved your father, and by this I mean Alex. Ben, he was so much like you, a tiger shifter, beautiful and good. He was my fated mate in every respect of the word. Unfortunately, my father didn't see it like that. He wanted nothing to do with Alex. He had decided that Richard was wealthy and respectable and they got on, so I had no say in it. Grandma fought for me, but she couldn't fight against her husband — you know how much the wolf world is still dictated to by its hierarchy. Yes, your grandfather was human, but his father had been a wolf shifter and he wanted to try and ensure that I had wolves when I had children, to carry on the *line of wolves in his family. It was faulty reasoning, but he was a powerful man, and what he said was law within our family.*

Breaking the news to Alex that I was not going to become fated mates with him and leave our town broke both our hearts, and in a moment of madness, we mated, risking everything. Alex was beaten for spoiling me and carried far away. I have no idea if he survived or not and I was forced into a union with Richard. I knew the child I was carrying wasn't Richard's and so did he. To save face, he agreed to say that you were his child and he would bring you up as his own, and I naïvely believed him.

Whilst you were little, we managed to make it work in our own way. Your grandma helped a lot, which she could do because by then your grandfather had died. I'm ashamed to have wished his death ever since he refused his consent to marriage with Alex. We had a suspicion that your animal would be a tiger, and we started making plans on how we could help you. Neither of us imagined what Richard would do when you began to shift.

I can understand he felt that my infidelity was a direct slur on him, but you were the innocent in it all. Unfortunately for everyone, he chose to target you, for he knew it would hurt me in a way that any attack on me would never do. He threatened that if you didn't leave, he would contact the type of people who would be interested in a tiger shifter being born to a wolf shifter.

I went cold at the words on the page. My mother must be referring to the same sort of people Kerry and Nathan had been fleeing from. There could be more than one group, but there was a distinct possibility that it was the same people. Unknowingly, my mother could have given me a lead which could prove helpful, but now it was too late. I continued to read.

I couldn't stand by and let you be treated like some sort of freak show, which Richard knew full well, so I agreed to whatever he wanted to do. He'd spent quite a bit of time causing ill feelings towards you in the village. I hated that he pretended you were an abomination, rather than that you were the result of a love match. I'm so sorry that you had to go through what you did. It was the only thing I felt I could do, to try and pretend that all was well, when it so clearly wasn't. At that point, I couldn't leave him. I didn't have the resources, and there was no way we could have uprooted your grandma, as she was in poor health.

Since he forced my hand and you were all but driven out of the village, I was determined that, although I couldn't give you the support I wanted to, I would leave you enough that you would never need to return to this part of the country ever again. Both your grandma and I put every penny we could away. I have been so proud of what you've achieved and wanted to show it in the only way I could – financially. I hope it will help set you up when you have a family. Don't think all marriages are as toxic as mine was – there are women out there who would love you as you deserve to be. Being a grandmother was something I longed for, but I knew your experience would affect your relationships. I don't know how many times I need to apologise before you start to roll your eyes, but believe me, from the moment I woke up to the moment I fell asleep, I was sending silent apologies in your direction.

I hope one day you can look back on some of your early years with a little happiness and hope you can understand why I've made the choices I have.

I love you, my boy. I have from the moment I knew you were growing inside of me, until I took my last breath. I couldn't have loved you more.

Mum xx

The letter fluttered to the worktop as I covered my face. For the first time in a long time, I let myself feel the emotions I'd tried so hard to suppress, which resulted in tears pouring down my face and my whole body shaking with sobs. I knew how restricting a pack could be when anything wasn't quite right; add to that a mean-spirited man and a foolish decision by my mother and it was a recipe for disaster.

She had tried to protect me in the only way she could in her circumstances. I felt a little sympathy for Richard – he would never be Dad to me from now on. I don't know when he'd started to threaten Mum with contacting people who would have been unscrupulous.

My thoughts were interrupted by a knock on the door. Richard had a certain rap he always used and

189

I knew it was him without opening the door or scenting him.

"You still here?" he asked without preamble. "It's been two weeks and the lads are wondering how long you're going to be sticking around for. They don't like your kind."

"Funny that they didn't mind so much when there were two of us," I responded.

"They want you gone. I want you gone."

I grabbed his arm and dragged him inside the house. I didn't really want him in this house, but I wouldn't be returning to it, so he couldn't tarnish any memories. Throwing him against the wall, I came up close.

"I want to ask you a few questions and then I'll leave," I said.

"Get your filthy claws off me!" he snapped. I could see he wanted to shift – his wolf was probably jumping at his ribcage to get to me, but it wouldn't win, a fact Richard knew full well.

Letting my claws show a little, I saw the swallow he took. Releasing him, I retracted my claws. I'd shown him what I was prepared to do, but I wasn't a bully like he was. I just needed to unnerve him enough to get some information out of him.

"Who was the group you were going to hand me over to in order to get rid of me?" It was satisfying to see the surprise on his face.

"Why do you want to know that?"

"That's of no concern. I want to know who they are, then I'll leave this place."

"I thought you'd want to know why I could never take to you," he sneered.

"Not interested." I shrugged. Again, it seemed I'd surprised him, and was it disappointment I could sense? I hoped so. I don't like bullies and refuse to give them what they want.

"I can't remember."

"That's a shame, because the longer it takes for you to recall who they are and how to contact them, the longer I intend staying. After all, this is my house now and it's lovely," I said, looking down the hallway.

"You hate this village as much as it hates you!"

"Maybe, but I want information more and I'm prepared to fight your cronies if it means I get to stay here." I wasn't a tiger cub any more; it would take dozens of wolves to take me down, something he knew. My bulky size was advantageous sometimes.

"You always were a damned nuisance."

"You have an easy way of getting rid of me for good. Once I've gone, I won't be coming back," I assured him.

"It was a man called William Boyd. He worked for a company called Corinthian. They were – I don't know if they're still in existence – a computing firm that acted as a front. They're based in Salisbury but have connections with the people who are interested in mutant shifters," Richard said.

I wanted to berate him for even thinking of putting me through whatever they would do to try and find out what I was, when I was just your average shifter, but I wouldn't give him the satisfaction of knowing that I cared.

"You can go now, safe in the knowledge that I'll be leaving very soon," I said, stepping back and opening the door, so he was free to leave.

"Good. Don't come back." Richard walked out the door and, without looking back, returned to his house.

Shutting the door, I immediately rang Eddie. "Hey, pal, could you look into a William Boyd for me, please? He worked at a company named Corinthian. It looks like it was a front for some tracking of shifters who can multi-shift," I explained. "He was there quite a while ago, so he might not be working there now, but anything you can find out would be great."

"Will do," Eddie said. "Have you spoken to Malc?"

"No," I answered, immediately alert.

"He rang me about half an hour ago, and to be honest, I've been debating whether or not to ring you myself. As it seems you are working on other things as well as sorting out your mum's estate, I suppose I should tell you."

"What's happened? Are Kerry and Nathan safe?"

"Yes. Kerry left the island nearly a week ago. There was an attack when she was on the mainland. She's ok," Eddie assured me quickly. "She's actually in your lodge, but she's hiding out there and I thought it was a good thing, just while things settled down."

"What's changed to cause you concern?" I demanded.

"Malc's call. Ring him, Ben."

"Will do. Thanks, Eddie. I'm glad you're watching Kerry."

"Constantly," Eddie assured me. "Oh, your car is parked at Aviemore station."

"Aviemore? But that's miles away from the lodge!"

"Yes. I think she was trying to put them off her scent," Eddie said.

"Bloody hell! What's been going on?" I demanded, not expecting an answer. "I'll ring Malc now. Bye, Eddie."

"I'll get on with enquiries about Corinthian," Eddie said before hanging up.

Malc answered on the third ring. "Hello, Ben."

His calm voice soothed me a little. "Hi. What's been happening? I believe there have been developments?"

"There certainly has," Malc said, before telling me all of what had happened when Kerry left the island. "I know you've had your friend on the job, but there's been one or two of us on the mainland, keeping an eye on your lodge."

"Thank you," I said. It was comforting to know Kerry hadn't been entirely on her own, even though she must have felt it. "What's made you contact Eddie today?"

"Our boat was attacked during the early hours of the morning," Malc said. "We thought the one who'd got away might have reported that we weren't worth the hassle, but it seems not."

"Where was the boat?" I dreaded him saying it was moored on the island, for that would suggest a breach in their security.

"Out in the cove. Don't worry, there's been no attempt to get on the island, but I'm suspecting they know we're here. Thankfully for us, the witches are extremely powerful and it would take a lot to breach the magic which has been set," Malc assured me.

"Even so..."

"We've increased the security and are taking the threat very seriously," Malc said, a smile in his voice at my worry. "We're all safe, but Kerry is a weak link and I'm not sure I could control Nathan if she were used as bait."

"No. He would put himself in danger," I agreed.

"I wanted to let Eddie know that I thought Kerry was vulnerable, even with our protection," Malc said. "We can't be there twenty-four hours and the moment she decides to leave..."

"It's ok. I'll be there later. I'm going to book a flight up, whatever it costs, and I'll protect her as much as she needs," I said.

"This is an organisation that doesn't give a fig about taking another's life," Malc cautioned. "They shot her brother in cold blood just because he was of no use to them any longer. Be careful."

"I will be," I assured him. "Thanks, Malc."

*

The flight passed quickly enough, but the forty-minute train journey from the airport to Aviemore and then the drive to my lodge seemed to take forever. All the time I kept thinking that I would arrive too late, that she'd have been attacked.

Seeing her car where we'd left it, I didn't know whether it was a good thing or bad. Climbing out of my car, I didn't stop to appreciate the clear air as I usually did when I arrived here; instead, I ran around to the front of the lodge and hammered on the door.

"Kerry, open the door!" I demanded, only just preventing myself from barging in.

I heard a scraping noise of something being dragged from the back of the door, and stepped back, ready to shift if needed.

Slowly, the door opened, and a very pale Kerry peeped around the crack. "Ben?" she asked, as if she couldn't believe I was there.

"Yes. Could you please let me in?" I asked, trying to sound calm. Opening the door wider, I closed and locked it as soon as I was in the lodge. "Can you please explain why you are in the middle of nowhere instead of being in a city, surrounded by people, when there's a madman on the loose?"

"A madman? The third person at the harbour?"

"It seems so, and you're here unprotected." I noticed the kitchen knife on the counter and I immediately crossed to her. "If anything had happened to you – why the bloody hell didn't you ring me to tell me what had happened? You kept saying you were fine in your texts."

"So did you," Kerry said. I hadn't touched her, but I longed to take her into my arms, to prove to myself that she was safe.

"What do you mean?"

As always, when she was concerned about something, she pushed her glasses up her nose before wrapping her arms around her middle. "I could tell something was going on, but didn't know whether it was me you wanted to distance yourself from, or if something unexpected had happened at home. I didn't want to bother you with what had gone on here."

Knowing she'd been worried, I felt a complete sleaze at being distant. I knew I had been. It was a conscious move on my part; not to be nasty – I just wasn't used to relying on anyone or turning to someone when I was hurting. "I'm sorry. There's a lot to tell you and it wasn't anything you'd done, just my inability to function like a normal human being," I admitted. "I've never been able to rely on others when I have personal problems, and I don't suppose it's been something you've done recently either. We're both daft," I said, touching her arm and sliding my hand until I held hers.

"Speak for yourself," Kerry said with a hint of a smile.

"I've missed you so much. I knew what I felt about you before I left and I was a bit afraid of it, but I missed you more than I imagined I would," I said. "And

I have a lot to tell you. I hope you've got some wine in here. I could really do with some."

"Sorry, all I've got left is tea or coffee and that will have to be black," she admitted with a rueful smile. "There were a few nights when my only comfort was a few glasses of wine."

"A kiss will make up for it," I said, pulling her gently towards me. When she didn't pull away, my grin spread. At last I could relax, for a little time anyway.

Chapter 18

Kerry

We'd talked long into the night, clearing the air between us and each telling the other what had happened since we'd parted. Finishing by admitting what we felt about each other had meant our conversation had turned to passion, which had been wonderful. Waking up with Ben's arms around me was a pleasure I hadn't expected to happen yesterday. It had been the best night's sleep I'd had since leaving the island and I felt better for it. I started to stretch, but stopped as Ben snuggled further into me.

"It's time to get up," I said, not trying to move away from his embrace.

"Not yet," he muttered into my hair.

I still felt the after effects of the late night so I could understand his reluctance. "Come on, lazy bones, that tiger of yours is going to need some exercise."

"Nope. He says he's quite content here with you," Ben responded.

"I think I just heard you purring," I laughed.

"Not me, him," he said. Groaning as his phone rang, he rolled over onto his back, reaching for his mobile. "Morning, Eddie," he said. "I'm going to put you on speakerphone so that Kerry can hear everything."

"Hello, Eddie," I said. I knew I was blushing, still being in bed with Ben. Even though Eddie couldn't see us, it just felt a little personal, especially without my glasses on. I reached for them and put them on, sitting up in bed. I felt less exposed with them on, plus I could gaze at Ben's body while I listened to Eddie.

"Morning. It seems you could have given us a lead yesterday, Ben. Corinthian definitely requires further exploration. On the surface, they look like a company which undertakes research for governments and businesses, all very above board and normal."

"But?" Ben asked.

"One or two of their staff have tried to be whistle-blowers and come forward with accusations of unethical work they take on for anyone who pays enough. Those same people have then disappeared off the radar," Eddie said.

"Killed?" I asked, feeling slightly sick.

"No proof of anything at the moment. They could have been paid off and be living on some Caribbean island somewhere, but they're definitely no longer in this country," Eddie admitted. "The name you gave is of a man who died about five years ago, Ben. No suspicious circumstances; heart attack and above board."

"I was hoping I could make contact with him and try to get into the organisation some way," Ben admitted.

I was going to object to his plan, but thankfully, Eddie spoke first. "This is too dangerous for you, or us as a team, to try and go storming in there, Ben. You would be a dead hero within minutes. A company that works with the dodgiest countries in the world doesn't like people coming in who might stir up trouble. I think you need to work out a way of keeping Kerry safe and the shifter community hidden. Choose your battles – going direct to the source isn't the way to win this."

"I intend keeping her safe, but how do we know that they won't send more men out to finish the job the others didn't complete?" Ben asked. I wanted to know the answer to the same question, but I didn't want to ask for fear I wouldn't like the response.

"I might have arranged a little diversion for them," Eddie said with a soft chuckle.

"What have you done?" Ben asked, a grin on his face.

"You remember my mum's best friend is a vampire?"

"Yy-es," Ben responded, obviously as confused as I was as to where this was going.

"Her husband is a mean so-and-so high up in the secret service, but he's also my godfather. I might have just had a chat with him and told him what was potentially going on in his area. He wasn't happy about it, not happy at all, especially as one of his best operatives is a shifter who can change into numerous forms. He's said he is going to both overtly and covertly make their life hell over the coming months. He aims to put them in such a position that they no longer want to work in the UK." Eddie sounded quite pleased with himself.

"And do you think that will work?" Ben asked.

"Let's put it this way – he has a lot of senior people in this country and abroad on speed dial. He's a man with a lot of influence and not one who you want to have working against you."

"You are brilliant, do you know that, Eddie? Most of the time, you terrify me, but today I am in awe, my friend. In complete awe."

"I like to be of service," Eddie said, an obvious smile in his voice.

"Thank you, Eddie," I said. I'd been listening in silence, and if Ben was in awe of his friend, I was absolutely astounded at what he could organise in such a short space of time.

"You're very welcome," Eddie said. "I'll keep you informed of any updates I get."

"Eddie, before you go, could I ask another favour, seeing as you've now got nothing to do?" Ben asked cheekily.

"You do know I am setting up all our surveillance systems for when Charlie and you decide we are good to go, don't you?" Eddie asked.

"Yes, but you're not out dating like you should be, so you have loads of spare time," Ben responded.

"I'm not going to comment on that last remark because Kerry is in the room and I don't swear in front of ladies. What is it you want?"

"Could you try to find out all you can about an Alexander Benjamin Ratchford? Please?" Ben asked.

"Of course. Anything in particular I should be looking for?"

"Just keep in mind that he's my natural father, but I want to know everything, good or bad."

There was a slight pause and then Eddie agreed to Ben's request and said his goodbyes.

Ben flopped back on the bed and I leaned across him and kissed him. "You're doing the right thing in trying to find him. You'll only wonder about him otherwise."

"I know, but it is slightly scary. It's potentially opening myself up for yet more parental rejection," Ben admitted.

"There's no guarantee of that, and at least you will have tried. Now for a far more mundane conversation. I need to return home and decide what to do – whether to try and find a job in this area, or have a long commute every school holiday to see Nathan," I said. It's all I'd been thinking of over the last few days. Well, that, and whether there was any future for Ben and me. I hadn't got far with either issue.

"What do you want to do?" Ben asked. He'd stiffened slightly and I was worried that I was going to spoil the new understanding we'd come to since last night.

"I don't know if I want to continue working in the bank. It's a good job, but it doesn't exactly give job satisfaction, and if these last few months have taught me anything, it's that life is too short to plod along," I admitted.

"You could come and live with me," Ben said quietly.

I paused before answering, the conversation I'd had with Bev ringing in my ears. "What about in your long-term future?"

"I don't understand what you mean."

"What we shared last night was wonderful and I think the world of you, I really do, but I know about fated mates. Bev said some shifters will only mate with their own kind." There. It was out in the open. I was now going to find out if my heart would be broken when Ben admitted that our 'thing' was only until he found his true mate.

Ben moved away slightly. "This is really hard to say."

My heart plummeted. "It's ok," I said, but I couldn't hide the choke in my voice. "I do understand about the needs of your animal and your heritage. Bev explained it."

Ben turned to me and grasped my hands. "Do you know how hard it is to try and hide my feelings when they are almost overwhelming? My animal – me – knew from the moment you followed Nathan out of the lodge that you were my fated mate. It's instinctive, primal even, but we know without doubt. I'd given up hope of ever finding mine, and when I did find her, there were two problems: you were having all sorts of trouble and weren't a shifter. Humans don't understand the overwhelming urge to perform the mating ceremony to secure our mate, to tell the world that you are mine. It's very caveman-like and would

203

have most modern women running for the hills. It makes me cringe, so goodness knows what you think about it," he said.

I could see the uncertainty in his face, the assumption that he'd said too much and that I'd react poorly, but I was singing inside. Trying to school my features into a bland expression, I touched his arm gently. "It is a bit archaic, isn't it?"

"Yes, but it's in our DNA and we can't avoid it," he answered dully.

"I think without meeting Malc and Bev, I might have been tempted to run a little distance, but I'm not sure I'd have completely run away. You see, I think you're my fated mate also. Yes, you're gorgeous to look at, which is a bonus, but from that first moment I also felt a pull to you; otherwise, you would have been kicked out of the lodge in no uncertain terms," I said. "Being able to watch how Bev and Malc interacted helped me to understand what it would be like to be joined for life on a deeper level than just by marrying. Theirs is an equal partnership – in some ways I'd say weighted towards Bev – but it was good to see them together."

Ben leaned towards me, mischief in his amber eyes. "Does this mean you intend to assert yourself?"

Laughing, I swatted him with my hand. "You wish."

"Oh, I do," Ben replied, kissing me briefly. "Does this mean you are happy to become my mate?"

"I am, but..."

"I was expecting a but," he said, his voice sad.

It was a surprise that someone who was strong, usually confident, and gorgeous to boot could be so insecure. "The but is just the speed at which things have happened. I've never felt so much about anyone else, but I don't want either of us to rush in and then change our minds," I admitted.

"I won't change mine," he assured me. "But I do appreciate why you feel it's very soon. It was one of the reasons I tried to give you some distance when I was away."

"I don't want us to be distant; I want to have the time to make sure this is right for us, when we haven't been trying to dodge my brother and his cronies and most of our attention has been focused on Nathan. I want to be like normal people who date, which I know won't be easy, as we live miles apart, with you moving down to the outskirts of London." I still lived in Manchester, and although he had an apartment there, I knew he was in the process of selling it to move to the south for his new business.

"Can I make one request, which might seem like it's going against what you've just said, but it isn't, honestly," Ben asked.

"Go on."

"Will you move south with me? Now, before you accuse me of racing ahead again, it would make sense because then we could have all the time in the world to get to know each other without the pressure of being backwards and forwards halfway across the country every weekend. With the new business, I expect I'll be working some weekends, and I don't want that impacting us."

"And what do I do for work?" I asked. I admit his proposal was very tempting. So much for me not rushing into things.

"Mum has left me enough money to be able to support us both for a long time if neither of us were working. Plus, there's my apartment, which I'm going to sell, Grandma's house and my own savings. You're looking at a rich man," Ben said with a grin.

"I'm not being a kept woman." My inner feminist was screaming at me at his words.

"You won't be; it won't take you a week before you're bored stiff and have found yourself a job, and I hope it pays well, because I don't mind being a kept man. At all."

"You are ridiculous."

"It has been said before. Now, before we get up, because you're starving me to death here, what do you say? Are we going to be mates in practice?"

"Yes, we are," I said, knowing that I would never need anyone other than Ben in my life. I was being cautious, but I knew in my heart that he was perfect for me.

Letting out a whoop, he grabbed and kissed me. Breaking the kiss, he smiled, all his joviality gone for the moment. "Thank you. I will spend my every waking moment convincing you that you've made the right decision. It might seem soon, but I know you are for me, Kerry."

I wanted to tell him I agreed with him and I loved him, but I held back a little. I had to be sure and so did he. "Good. Now come on, we have some packing to do. It's time to join the rest of the world."

Chapter 19

Ben

I knew we were being followed the moment the large black 4x4 moved in two cars behind me on the dual carriageway. We'd only been driving for half an hour and there was someone on our tail. I hated that Kerry had insisted on driving her own car, and although she was in front of me, I wasn't happy that we were separated.

Eddie picked up on the second ring. "I see you're on the move," he said.

"I'm glad you're keeping an eye on us," I said. "There's a car on our tail. It looks like a BMW, black, with tinted windows, so stereotypical. Can you see if there's a route which will take Kerry out of their reach whilst they follow me?"

"Kerry isn't in the car with you?" Eddie asked.

"No. Are you not tracking her?"

"According to my system, her car is still parked outside your lodge," Eddie said.

"Damn! That means someone traced the tracker I placed on her vehicle. I only put it there this morning. I didn't detect anyone and neither did my tiger." I was blazing that they'd managed to get so close to us without my animal knowing.

"Did you go out today?"

"Briefly, for the shortest run. They must have done it then, but I can't understand why there was no trace of them when I returned. I should have picked something up."

"They're very good."

"Worryingly so," I admitted. "So much for my wish to get Kerry out of their way. They're approaching from the outside. I'm going to try and run them off the road."

"Be careful," Eddie said.

Ringing Kerry quickly, I had to make a snap decision. I didn't want to frighten her, but I also needed her to keep herself safe.

"Missing me already?" she teased as she answered my call.

"Always. Kerry, I need you to promise me something," I said, getting to the point. I could see the car gaining on me even as I spoke.

"What's wrong?"

"We're being followed, which I'm going to do something about, but I need you to promise me that no matter what happens, you won't stop," I said.

"You're expecting me to leave you behind and drive on?" Kerry asked in disbelief.

"That's exactly what I want you to do. I'll sort this, but I don't want to be worrying about you."

"Ben, the last time they caught up with us, they had guns."

"And I have a superb healing ability and sharp claws."

"But—"

"Please, Kerry. I need you to promise me this." The car was just about level with the rear of my car. I would need to act soon.

"Be careful," Kerry said. "I can see the car; it's the one which was at the side of the harbour. I'll get out of the way, I promise."

I hated that she wasn't with me. I didn't care if it was caveman-like – I wanted to protect her. "Thanks. Drive as fast as you can. Bye, Kerry."

Waiting until the car was level with the rear door, I moved out into the other lane, trying to push the vehicle off the road. The scrape of metal on metal made me wince, and my tiger's claws started to appear. "Not yet, buddy," I said to my tiger. "Your time will come, but I need the flexibility of my fingers for this part." Obligingly, he complied, and I kept the pressure on, slowly forcing the car over onto the verge at the side of the road. I was thankful that this was a quiet stretch of road; the danger to other vehicles would have stopped me from being so reckless if there had been any nearby.

Just when I thought he would have no option other than to go onto the verge, the car seemed to spring forward and edged further in front of mine. There was no subtleness in the next move – I was rammed hard from the left, which sent me careening into the verge on the opposite side of the dual carriageway. My front wheels came to rest in a small ditch.

Slamming the car into reverse, I cursed loudly and stood on the accelerator, hoping that there was enough traction to get me out of the ditch. Thankfully, luck was on my side in that regard, and the car jolted backwards at speed. A couple of cars were passing by now and blared horns at me, swerving to avoid me, but luckily, there still weren't too many vehicles on the road.

I'd lost precious seconds, and swearing to myself, I set off in pursuit. The car had almost caught up with Kerry, which caused me to lift myself out of my seat as I pressed the pedal to the floor, demanding even more speed out of my car.

Eddie called, and I answered without saying a word. I was concentrating. "You went off-road," he said.

"Only slightly. He's caught up with Kerry and we're on a hillside. If he pushes her over, I can't see how far the drop is!" I shouted. "Oh, dear God!"

It was as if the whole world had stopped, and all I could see was the black monster of a vehicle pushing Kerry's car, side on. Even an expert driver would have struggled to keep control of the car when that happened, but the speed at which Kerry was travelling made the car slew dangerously. I knew the moment she'd lost control, as the car seemed to lurch once and then spun in a full circle before careening off the road.

"Eddie, get help! She's gone over!" I screamed at my friend.

Not letting my speed up, I rammed into the back of the car, which had slowed to see the results of its actions. The driver didn't seem overly concerned, but jumped out of the vehicle as it bumped along the verge, not waiting until the vehicle stopped as it followed a different descent than Kerry's had.

Using his bonnet as a shield, he fired a shot at me. It ricocheted off the car, but I slammed on the brake, not caring that he would have the advantage over me. It would be short-lived.

Shifting before I'd got out of the car, my tiger bounded back towards the vehicle. I didn't care if anyone in a passing car saw a tiger bounding down a dual carriageway; I'd sort that problem out later. I was desperate to look for Kerry – there had been no fire, so that was something. I needed to reach the gunman before he could turn his attention to her.

Bounding over to him, I felt the bullets the moment they hit my body, but I didn't stop. I didn't care whether I survived or not, but there was one thing for sure – he wasn't going to.

Leaping over the bonnet of the car, my mouth closed around the gunman's throat, cutting off the scream he was about to utter. I never thought killing was the answer to anything, but in this instance, I let my tiger do what his instinct urged him to do.

Turning the moment the body slumped to the floor, I headed over the brow the road was built on and saw Kerry's car halted by a large tree. The airbags had been deployed, but from my angle, I couldn't see whether she was still in the car or not.

Running down the hillside, I could feel the loss of blood from my wounds. I needed to shift to enable the healing process to start, but I could tell the bullets were still inside. That would prevent the healing process from being completed, although in human form, I wouldn't lose as much blood, as the shift would help stem the flow, but I didn't care about shifting – my only urge was to get to Kerry.

Reaching her, I licked her and she moaned slightly. She was alive! That's all my tiger needed to know before I shifted and started to check her over.

There were cuts on her face, especially around the nose, where the air bag had pushed her glasses onto her face. One of the lenses of the glasses was cracked. Her hands looked to have minor injuries, but there didn't seem to be anything serious. Moving down her body, she moaned in pain when I reached her ribs. I didn't know if they were broken or bruised, but she'd hit the tree with some force; I doubted it would ever stand tall again. The front of her car had crumpled badly, and although she wasn't trapped, one glance at her and I could see she'd broken one of her legs. It was probably a good thing she was unconscious.

I spoke to her the whole time, even though she probably couldn't hear me. I didn't want to leave her to retrieve my phone and get help – I had to rely on the fact that Eddie would have contacted the emergency services.

Bending over as a wave of nausea and dizziness passed over me, I realised I was slowly being covered in my own blood. Being naked meant there was nothing to soak the blood up, and it must have looked like some bloody murder scene.

The dizziness wasn't passing, but I could hear car doors slamming in the distance. I stood up to go and meet the vehicles, but the blackness took over before I'd taken a single step.

*

I felt myself being hauled onto something and there was a comforting presence nearby. I vaguely wondered if I was dying and my mum had come to get me. The thought of dying didn't scare me, apart from that I was worried about Kerry.

Consistently trying to call out to her, I heard voices in the distance. They were deep voices; none of them sounded like my mother. I paused, trying to work out who they could be. My mind was sluggish and unresponsive, but I was grateful for the person who stood next to me, their hand on my shoulder in a gesture of comfort.

I wanted to fall into the blackness, but worry about Kerry kept me trying to push to consciousness. Kerry – I needed to get to her. What if the voices I could hear belonged to the people who wanted Nathan? I hadn't checked the car for any others; I'd just been focused on the driver.

Trying with all my might to reach Kerry, the voices around me started to chatter. Their tone sounded urgent and I distinctly heard someone saying,

"He's trying to get to her. We need to sedate him or he's going to kill himself."

They were stopping me from getting to Kerry. I growled out in anger and pushed against the hands which were holding me down, but it was of no use. I didn't feel the needle going in, but I felt the fluid rushing through my veins and then everything went black.

Chapter 20

Kerry

I'd never been so frightened in my life as when I lost control of the car. I couldn't focus on a thing as it spun, and then when it crested the brow of the grass verge and I could see the drop at the other side, I truly believed at that moment that I was going to die. Seeing the occasional tree on the hillside stretching out before me, I realised they might be the thing which had the possibility of saving me. I yanked on the steering wheel, hoping that the steering shaft hadn't been broken in the crash into the verge. It seemed someone was looking after me that day, because the wheels moved and I aimed for the tree.

Bracing for impact, I thought of Ben and Nathan, hoping with all my heart that I would survive to see them again. I have no idea how something which happened so fast and at speed could feel like such a long time, but I heard the crash and felt the force of the airbag before passing out.

I came round with a cry of agony. They were trying to remove me from the car and it was causing such pain in my leg. Oh my word, I'd never felt anything like it, but there was something else – I knew Ben was hurt. I couldn't explain how I knew that, but without a doubt, I was convinced he was injured.

Calling out to him, someone came and put their hand on my shoulder and shushed me. "But Ben," I sobbed at the stranger.

"He's being cared for. We need to get you out of the car," he said gently. His tone was reassuring and my panic started to ease a little. I dipped in and out of consciousness, but started to try to escape when I heard the noise of a helicopter. The pain might be excruciating, but I worried that after all that had happened, I was going to be kidnapped by the people who had been working with Neil.

"Let me go! Let me go!" I started to struggle, which made me want to vomit, as the pain almost overwhelmed me, but I had to try and escape, however futile my struggle was.

"Easy there," came the same gentle voice that had been nearby throughout the whole situation. "It's the air ambulance; we need to get you both to the hospital and this is the quickest way of doing it."

"I was being chased," I started to try to explain.

"It's ok, don't fret," the man soothed. "No one is chasing you now. You're going to be taken to hospital and looked after. I'm a police officer and will need to talk to you at some point, but no one is going to hurt you."

"And Ben?" I asked.

"He's being looked after too."

"Is he ok?"

"He'll be fine. He needs a minor procedure that can be done at the hospital. Don't worry, you'll both be ok."

"Are you coming with us? Please? I don't want them to get to us."

He smiled. "I can do, but you are surrounded by friends."

The activity around me increased as we were loaded into the helicopter. I was jolted, and the pain in my ribs made me faint once more.

*

Coming around, I was in a hospital bed in a private room. I remembered bits of the journey and the pain. My leg was in traction and my arms were bandaged. I had some padding on part of my face and wasn't wearing my glasses. I looked at the bedside locker, but there was no sign of them.

"Hello, sleepyhead." The voice of the stranger disturbed my search for my glasses.

"You stayed with me," I said.

"Of course. I couldn't resist your appeal," he said with a smile. "And it meant I had a ride in a helicopter."

"How's Ben? Do you know?"

"He's fine, just sleeping off his minor surgery," he said. "He's in the room next to yours. I'm sure he'll be in when he wakes up. He was insistent about being close to you, even though he was barely conscious."

"Good," I said, closing my eyes a little. "I think I've had some drugs," I said, feeling heavy-lidded.

"Yes, you were in a lot of pain."

"I can't find my glasses…"

"They've been taken to be repaired. The local optician has said he'll get it sorted as soon as he can. I'm afraid they were badly damaged."

"You said you are with the police?"

"Yes, and if you're happy to speak to me, I can take your statement. I was first on the scene."

I didn't think to question who had called in the crash; I was just glad the police had got there quickly. "Ben's a police officer."

"Is he? That's interesting. Would you like me to take a statement when you've had some more sleep?"

"Yes, please. I'm very tired."

"That's fine. I'll go and get a coffee and see you later."

"Are you sure that man can't get to us here?" I asked.

"No. Ben made sure he won't be attacking anyone again."

"Oh dear, I hope he won't get in trouble."

"No, he won't. Not if I have anything to do with it, anyway."

"Do I know you? You seem familiar."

He smiled at me. "No. We've never met before."

I drifted off to sleep, thanking our lucky stars that this police officer had been the first to find us.

*

The next time I awoke, I felt more refreshed, and although still in pain, especially when I breathed, I felt better when I was handed a pair of glasses. They weren't my pair, but they were the same prescription. It was nice to have the world in clearer focus.

The police officer was sitting in my room and I smiled at him. "Have I been asleep long?"

"A couple of hours, but you look a healthier colour for it."

"I'm ready to give you my statement now," I said.

"That's good." He proceeded to take me through everything which had happened from leaving the island. I'd been worried about the questions which might arise about the island, but he didn't ask anything which could cause me discomfort. At the end of the statement, he got me to sign what he'd written and then stood to go. "I have an officer sitting with Ben, but I wanted to take his statement too."

"Can I see him?"

"After I've taken the statement, yes."

I wasn't happy with not seeing Ben yet. It had felt too long, and I began to wonder if everything was ok. "He is next door, isn't he? And he's well?"

"He's absolutely fine, and by all accounts as desperate to see you as you are to see him. You must think a lot of each other."

"We do." I didn't want to start talking about fated mates. I wasn't sure what this officer's opinion was on shifters.

"Now just relax, there's nothing for you to worry about."

"Police training is obviously very good. You're just like Ben, great in a crisis," I said.

I received a curious expression at my words before he left me alone. I wished I had my mobile on me; I wanted to check on Nathan, but it seemed nothing, apart from my glasses, had been brought from the crash site. I just hoped Nathan wasn't trying to get through to me.

Dozing off again, I hoped Ben would be in soon.

Chapter 21

Ben

I was pacing the room like the caged tiger I was. I'd been banned from going through to Kerry until we'd had our statements taken. I think only the fact that the young officer who had the misfortune of sitting in the room with me was more afraid of his senior officer than he was of me kept him in his seat and insisted that I hadn't to interrupt the interview going on in the next room. I had to give him credit, because my beast was pulsating anger off me and it took a strong person not to respond in a submissive manner.

Eventually, the other officer entered the room and I felt like the room was spinning. I knew this man. I had no idea how, but I knew him. Standing with arms folded, I waited as he closed the door after dismissing the officer. He stood, an amused look on his face, as he observed my aggressiveness.

"Hello Ben. Shall we get your statement out of the way first of all?"

"There's nothing else to discuss, is there?" I asked.

"We can get to that. If you'd like to take a seat, we can start at the beginning," he said. I knew what he was doing – diffusing the situation, being pleasant, but not overly friendly. I'd used the method lots of times myself, which annoyed me even further.

There was no point in being belligerent about it, so I sat and started my story from when we'd set off from my lodge. It didn't take long, and when I'd finished, he put the top on his pen in a precise way and popped it into the top pocket of his shirt.

"What about the man I left dead on the road?" I asked.

"It will be reported that he died in the accident," he answered. "Now that's out of the way, I think it's time to get down to more interesting topics, don't you?"

"I want to see Kerry," I said.

"I want to know why you have a driving licence in one name and a birth certificate in another," he said amiably.

"Lots of people use different names than what they're born with," I said with a shrug. I'd forgotten I'd put my real birth certificate in my wallet.

"True, but not everyone has my name against the title of father, next to the mother's name, which just so happens to be the woman who I wanted to be my mate," he responded.

I paused.

"You're my father? You're Alexander Ratchford?" I asked in complete disbelief.

"It would seem so. I can see your animal has recognised me to some extent, just as mine recognised you at the crash site. I didn't know a child had been created when we paired."

"Having unprotected sex was irresponsible when you knew there were objections against the match," I pointed out.

"I agree, but that's what happens when you're young, in love and feel like you're taking part in some sort of Romeo and Juliet tragedy, just with shifter packs instead of humans. How is your mother?"

"She died recently." He faltered, unable to hide the stricken expression on his face, and I felt some remorse. "It was sudden, I think."

"You think?" he asked, schooling his features into a blander expression, clearly controlling the shock he felt.

"We hadn't been close in recent years."

"That surprises me. She wanted a family to love; she talked often of how big our family was going to be," he said, reminiscing about his past.

"I wouldn't normally divulge this, but I suppose you need to understand how her life changed when it became clear to the man who I thought was my father that it could no longer be hidden that I wasn't his. He punished us both when I started to shift and threatened to harm me in a way that he wouldn't be doing the dirty work, but wouldn't have been pleasant for me," I admitted. "She pushed me away to try to stop my being caught up in something which could destroy me, and although I didn't understand her motivation, our home life was difficult to the point I was happy to go."

"He hurt her," he growled. "I'll kill him."

"I wouldn't risk your career for him. He really isn't worth it." It was strange having this conversation as if we were two acquaintances, and not reacting to the realisation that we were father and son. "Shall we start again?" I asked. "I'm Ben and I believe I'm your son."

I held out my hand and he shook it before grasping me in a hug. "I would have found you if I had known anything about you. I never thought I'd be lucky enough to have a son; you've just made an old man very happy," he said gruffly.

His words touched me deeply, which surprised me, but I suppose I'd longed for acceptance by my father, who would never have given it to me, no matter how hard I tried to please him. Yet this man had accepted me instantly as his son and seemed happy about it. It was natural to be affected by his sentiment. "You're not that old – you're still in the job," I said, trying to lighten the mood a little.

"That's only because they changed the retirement age, and now I'll be in the job until I'm on a walking frame," he responded.

"You must have been young when you got together with my mother."

"I was. We both were."

"Did you ever meet anyone else?" I asked.

"No. There was no one else for me once I'd found my mate."

"I know how that feels," I admitted.

He smiled at me. "She's human. Does she know how mixed up her life is going to be by attaching herself to a shifter?"

"I think so, some of it anyway," I said, frowning. It still worried me a little that things were moving very fast for Kerry.

"I'm happy to listen if you want to talk," Alex said.

"What? Meet you for the first time and then start unburdening myself on you? That's not a good start, is it?"

"It would make me feel as if I was being useful to you, to try and make up for not being there when you really needed support," Alex said with a growl.

His words touched me. I had longed for support, and in other circumstances I would have received it. It helped to ease some of the pain I still felt, and I decided to take him up on his offer. I told him about all that had happened, which had brought me into contact with Kerry and her own complicated life since Nathan's development.

"We know about the island," he said. "Well, the Highland shifter community does. We would never try to go there, but we do help out from time to time if they have a problem with someone trying to reach them."

"They seem to have a network of support, which is great for them with people like Corinthian working to harm them. I'd love to see them brought down. What they're doing is wrong on every level."

"Be careful. I don't want to lose you as quickly as I found you," he said. "Now I think it's time you went to check on that girl of yours."

We both stood and I looked at him closely. "I can see a resemblance between us."

"Yes. You gave me a bit of a shock when I found you at the crash site. I knew instantly there was some connection between us, but I couldn't figure out what it was. When your personal items had been brought to me from your car and I went through your wallet, I thought it was some kind of joke at first, that a man with the same name as me had fathered a child with either your mother or a woman of the same name. I was being stupid when the bloody obvious was staring me in the face."

"Can we keep in touch?" I asked. I knew what he'd said and the way he'd acted, but the inner child in me still expected rejection.

"Of course. Now that I know you exist, I will want to make sure you're ok in the future," he answered.

"I'd like to take it slowly, though. I'm a bit raw after everything that I've found out. I'm sorry if that hurts you."

"What hurts me is that I wasn't able to do anything to protect you or your mother. I'd have ripped him apart if I'd known how he was with you both. It's going to be hard coming to terms with the fact that my life could have been so different if I'd known about you. I wouldn't have made the choices that I have." He looked genuinely upset and I wondered about his life. It seemed all three of us had been affected by the moment of madness in which I'd been created. I wanted to question him, but knew now was not the right time – I needed to see Kerry, and that feeling was overwhelming any others which were swirling in the pit of my stomach.

"It's over now." I moved to the door. "I'll look forward to seeing you later, but I want to check on Kerry."

*

I'd climbed on the bed to be as close to Kerry as I could. I wanted to enfold her in an embrace and never let her go again. She looked so pale, tired and in pain, but she'd smiled when I walked through the door. That was the only encouragement I'd needed to join her on the uncomfortable hospital bed. She had objected, but had snuggled into me as much as she could.

We'd gone over what had happened, and a few times, I had to retract my claws as my beast became angry at what had happened. Kerry had stroked my fur-covered hands, and my tiger had responded, calming down.

I smiled at her, kissing her nose. "It seems you have both of us equally under your spell. Are you sure you aren't some sort of witch?"

"I wish I was, because I'd definitely be using a spell to get us both out of here and somewhere away from everyone," she responded.

"Does that mean you've had a change of heart and are going to move in with me?"

"Are you not sick of the trouble I bring? I'd be running for the hills if I were you."

"I'd never run away from you." I smiled at her. "I know it's sudden, but I'm surer of this than I've ever been of anything else." I loved the way she smiled at me and gently kissed my cheek, her touch soft and tender.

"So am I," she smiled. "After what's happened, there's not a doubt in my mind that we are meant to be together, and I want it more than I'd thought possible. When I thought you were injured or worse, I couldn't face the thought of not being with you all the time. It felt as if I would never be whole without you by my side."

"Are you saying what I think you're saying?" I asked, blood pounding in my ears.

"That I believe we're fated mates in your world and soul mates in mine? Yes, that's what I'm saying and I'm happy about it," she admitted.

"Are you sure? You might change your mind again once the shock has worn off," I cautioned. I wanted her more than anything, but I also needed her to want to commit to me for the right reasons.

"I'm perfectly sure," she answered, kissing me.

We were disturbed by a cough in the doorway, and reluctantly parted. A police officer stood in the open doorway, smiling in apology.

"Sorry to disturb you, but I believe you were in two of the three cars involved in the road traffic accident this morning on the A9?" he asked.

"We were," I answered.

"You've been hard to find."

"I don't understand. We were taken by air ambulance to this hospital," I said. I moved off the bed, but didn't move away from Kerry, holding her hand. Something the police officer had said, or the way he looked, set me on the alert.

"I don't know who brought you here, but it wasn't the emergency services. Until I questioned the nurses, we thought another car had driven you here. It's taken so long because we thought you'd gone to the hospital in Inverness," he said.

"Which hospital are we at?" I'd never thought to ask where we were.

"Forth Valley Royal Hospital near Falkirk. You didn't know?"

"No. We came by helicopter, both unconscious," I said.

"Do you feel well enough to go over what happened?" the officer asked.

"We've had statements taken by the police officer who was at the scene, an Alex Ratchford," I said, feeling sickened at what I could see unfolding.

"I'll radio through, but as far as I'm aware there's been no one else assigned to track you down and find out what went on. It was a pretty bad crash scene. Excuse me for a moment; the radios don't work well inside these buildings," the officer said, stepping outside the room and moving down the corridor.

Kerry looked at me in alarm. "What does it mean? Is he a fake police officer?"

"I don't know for sure, but I don't think so," I answered, switching my phone on, which Alex had given me, along with my wallet.

The moment the phone connected to the nearest aerial, it almost bounced out of my hand with messages of concern from Charlie and Eddie. I didn't answer any of them, preferring to ring Eddie instead.

"Hey, Ben, are you ok?" he asked as soon as he'd answered.

"We'll live. Eddie, did you call the emergency services? Did you arrange a helicopter to bring us to the hospital?" I asked.

"Yes, I rang the emergency services, but they were very dubious about what I was telling them, but I didn't arrange a helicopter. Why would I do that?"

"It doesn't matter for now. Another question for you – did you find anything out about Alex Ratchford?"

Eddie paused. "I did. I was hoping to see you before I told you, but there's obviously something going on up there, so here goes. Alex Ratchford was asked to resign from a Scottish police force about ten years ago. It was stated that he was working for another company whilst also working for the police and there could be some conflict of interest."

"What company was it?" But I knew. I didn't need to ask.

"Corinthian."

"Damn it," I cursed. "And we've just told him everything about the island. I've got to get in touch with Malc. Sorry to cut you off, Eddie, but I need to contact Malc – the island's safety might have been compromised."

"Stay safe, Ben, and please don't do anything rash," Eddie appealed before we said our goodbyes.

Immediately ringing Malc, I looked at Kerry. She looked as stricken as I probably did. I quickly explained to Malc what had happened, but instead of the anger I expected, he was quite calm.

"They'll already know about the island," he assured me. "We're not naïve enough to think otherwise. When I said some serious spells were protecting us, I meant it. Off the island, we might be vulnerable, but on the island, we are secure. I'll send a message out to everyone nonetheless and we'll certainly be on our guard when leaving the island, but don't worry – we face this every day, Ben, and have always done."

"I'm sorry," I apologised again before ringing off. Sitting down, I ran a hand through my hair. "I knew there was something not quite right, but I was so giddy at finding my father and pleased that he seemed to like me that I was blinded by everything else."

"I didn't know he was your father and yet I trusted him," Kerry pointed out. "Can he be found?"

"I don't know, but perhaps this officer can help," I said as the officer returned to our room.

He listened as I explained everything, including Alex being my father and who he worked for. "I'll send out a call to my superiors. This goes beyond reporting a road traffic accident," he said, once more leaving us alone.

A nurse passed him in the doorway and came over to me. "I've been given this note for you," she said. "The police officer asked for it to be given to you as soon as he left, but I'm afraid I had to attend to another patient." She handed me a folded piece of paper and left the room.

"What does it say?" Kerry asked.

"I'm almost frightened to read it," I admitted.

"Do you want me to look first?" she offered.

"Thank you, but no. Let's get this over with," I answered, opening the paper.

Dear Ben,

You will know very soon who I really am working for. We had been monitoring you from a distance, leaving one operative nearby. At that point, I had no idea who you were; Kerry was the focus of our attention. It was only when I reached the crash site that it became clear you were my son, and I admit that it sent me into a spin.

I was to deliver Kerry to headquarters and she would be used to get Nathan off the island, but I couldn't. I could see, even in both your confused states, that you were fated mates – the way you were concerned about each other, the worry driving you further than you would normally go. You took six bullets and kept going to get to Kerry. I couldn't separate you like I'd been parted from your mother, so I arranged to bring you both to the hospital, when I should have taken Kerry and left you by the roadside. There will be consequences to my actions, but I don't care about that. There was no way I was leaving you behind.

I needed to know what you knew about our operation, and for that reason, I took your statements. You are no longer a threat to us, and I give you my word that the island is under no increased threat from you, trusting me with everything. We've known about the island since the beginning and are aware of its defences.

It's true when I said to you that I would have made different choices if I'd known about you, and I hope that you can believe those words, because I would have done. I got involved with Corinthian because my sister, your aunt, was a multi-shifter and Corinthian got hold of her. She only lasted a year before her dead body was found. I decided then that I would bring them down at whatever cost to myself.

I will be signing this letter, so if you don't believe what I've said, all you need to do is to send this through to Corinthian and I will be a dead man. I shall accept it if you do. I know I will have hurt you by deceiving you, and for that I am sorry. Please don't get involved with them. I am going to tell them that Kerry died in the hospital and give them false paperwork to prove it. It's all I can do to try to protect her and her nephew. She will be safe once they see the documentation. They won't follow you because you don't hold the sway she has over getting her nephew off the island. You will be safe to be together.

Please be happy, Ben. Live your best life, and I can only hope that one day you can forgive me. If I manage to survive, I hope we might meet in better circumstances and have a beer or three. I can't believe that I helped to create someone as amazing as you seem to be.

Take care and be safe, son.
Best wishes
Alex Ratchford.

When I looked at Kerry, she was wiping her eyes. "Don't, you'll have me blubbing," I said, my voice croaky.

"He's a good guy, Ben," she said with a sniff.

"It could be another set of lies," I responded.

"Yes. It could, but it doesn't sound like it. Ben, he could have taken us in. He's put himself at risk and it's because he realised he was your father. A dad who cares for you from the moment he saw you," she said. I glanced at her and she smiled at me. "I know your innermost wishes. Believe in the words he's said. You could have a future with him."

"If he survives." I wanted to believe in him as much as I wanted Kerry for my mate, but I was afraid to trust his words after what had happened.

"It's time for us to take the opportunity and live our lives to the full, hoping that he and Eddie's godfather work to bring the company down," she said.

"We'll need to keep you safe, though. There might still be a threat towards you."

"We'll be careful, as Malc and the rest of the islanders will be. As he's said before, they're used to this," she said. "I refuse to let it blight our lives, although I won't take any unnecessary risks just in case."

"I can't stand the thought of you being at risk," I admitted.

"Promise me you aren't going to go in all guns blazing now you know your father is involved."

Moving back over to her, I wrapped her in my arms. "I can promise you that. I can't undermine any work which is already being planned. I'll have to be patient, but I want to convince Charlie and Eddie that we keep Corinthian in our sights, just in case we can do something to help at some point in the future," I said. It would be hard to accept that I couldn't tackle Corinthian, but I knew my limitations, and taking on a company was too big for one person, even three if I managed to convince Charlie and Eddie that we should do something about them. For once in my life, I was going to let someone else worry about the bigger picture while I enjoyed the chance at a happy life. I didn't know if I would be able to see my father again, but Kerry was right – he'd protected me when it had counted and that meant a lot. It would have to do for the moment.

"That I can cope with because Charlie and Eddie both seem far more reasonable and less fiery than you are," Kerry said.

Laughing, I looked at her, my mate, the woman I was going to spend the rest of my life with, bringing up as many children as she would agree to, creating a happy, noisy family home with. "You have no idea about those two. They make me look meek and mild," I said.

"In that case, I pity the women they end up with," Kerry said.

"So do I. They'll definitely have their hands full if they want to secure Charlie and Eddie."

And they really did.

The End

Order Charlie's story here:- Taming the Beast

https://www.amazon.com/dp/B094114FYF

https://www.amazon.co.uk/dp/B094114FYF

https://www.amazon.de/dp/B094114FYF

https://www.amazon.ca/dp/B094114FYF

https://www.amazon.com.au/dp/B094114FYF

Books by Amelia Hopegood

The Reluctant Witch – Book 1 in the Imperfect Witch Series

https://www.amazon.com/dp/B08FHCX565
https://www.amazon.co.uk/dp/B08FHCX565

The Avenging Witch – Book 2 in the Imperfect Witch Series

https://www.amazon.com/dp/B08FGHKBGN
https://www.amazon.co.uk/dp/B08FGHKBGN

The Fated Witch – Book 3 in the Imperfect Witch Series

https://www.amazon.com/dp/B08N1D2MD9
https://www.amazon.co.uk/dp/B08N1D2MD9

Releasing the Beast – Book 1 in the Imperfect Shifter Series

https://www.amazon.com/dp/B08W9Q2VLN
https://www.amazon.co.uk/dp/B08W9Q2VLN

Taming the Beast – Book 2 in the Imperfect Shifter Series

https://www.amazon.com/dp/B094114FYF
https://www.amazon.co.uk/dp/B094114FYF

About the Author

Thank you so much for reading my first story in the Cozy Mystery/Paranormal world. I love my characters and hope you did too.

You can send comments, or message me here:- https://www.facebook.com/Amelia-Hopegood-100408568342178/ or please follow me on my Amazon author page.

If you would like to receive notifications from me when new releases come out, please email amelia@ameliahopegood.co.uk I promise to never send out newsletters, or spam. You will only ever hear from me to let you know if there's something important to tell. Just send the email, with 'subscribe' in the heading and I'll do the rest. If you ever decide that you want to unsubscribe, just send 'unsubscribe' in the heading and again, I'll do the rest! I want to keep this as simple as possible for all of us!

If you have enjoyed this book, please could you spend a few moments leaving a review? They are vital for independent authors like myself, especially one just setting out. It's a scary journey being an indie author, but I have loved the process so far and hope it came across in the story.

Thank you for your support!
Kind regards
Amelia

www.ingramcontent.com/pod-product-compliance
Lightning Source LLC
Chambersburg PA
CBHW050035180626
46810CB00002B/721